D0867004

FLOUR

The Babysitter Chronicles is published by
Stone Arch Books,
A Capstone Imprint
1710 Roe Crest Drive,
North Mankato, Minnesota 56003
www.mycapstone.com

Cataloging-in-Publication data is available on the LIbrary of Congress website.

ISBN: 978-1-4965-2756-1 (library binding)
ISBN: 978-1-4965-2760-8 (eBook PDF)

Summary: When Bri is asked to babysit for her crush's younger siblings, she lets her interest in getting the boy distract her from her responsibilities.

Designer: Veronica Scott
Cover illustration: Tuesday Mourning
Image credits: Shutterstock: Guz Anna, design element, Marlenes, design element, Woodhouse, design element, Vector pro, design element; Capstone Studio, pg. 157

Printed in Canada
102015 009223FRS16

The
BABYSITTER
Chronicles
Bri's
Big
Crush
Melinda Metz
STONE ARCH BOOKS
a capstone imprint

Want to stop a toddler tantrum? Get goofy, and make them giggle instead!

Chapter 1

He's about to Hulk out!

McCoy's little hands curled into fists. He sucked in a huge breath of air and prepared for an epic screech. Once the three-year-old got started on a tantrum, it would be impossible to stop him. He'd have to exhaust himself, and McCoy didn't exhaust easily.

Brianna Wei calculated the distance to the living room sofa, where she'd left what she called her Mary Poppins bag. It was stocked with a bubble blower and bubble solution, sock puppets, a kazoo, and other tantrum-busters. *Way too far away,* Bri decided.

She swooshed her finger through the smear of ketchup left on her dinner plate and started drawing red whiskers on her face. McCoy blinked. His mouth was open, ready for screaming, but no sound came out. Bri quickly finished the whiskers and let out a long meow.

McCoy blinked again, hands still fisted, mouth still open. It could go either way.

Bri began to sing. "I'm a little kitty, nice and sweet. These are my whiskers . . ." She pointed to the ketchup on her face. ". . . these are my feet." She waved her hands. "When I go out hunting, mice beware. Or you might just get a scare!" She popped her fingers wide.

McCoy blinked once more and giggled.

Yeah! Super Babysitter triumphs over Hulk again! McCoy had clearly forgotten the unfairness of being denied a second after-dinner cupcake when he "really, really, really, really" wanted one. Bri smoothed her straight black hair and smiled.

"Again!" he cried.

Bri launched into the song again. Then she taught it to McCoy, who insisted on his own ketchup whiskers. They crawled around the house pretending to be kittens until bath time.

After one bath, two games of Candy Land (Bri cheated a little to let him win one), and three bedtime books, she sprayed the closet with Monster Away (air freshener with a special label Bri made) and turned out the light.

She headed to the kitchen. She knew McCoy would be asking for a drink in a few minutes, so she took out a sippy cup. Now that he was three, sippies were for bedtime water only. The rest of the time, he drank from big-boy plastic glasses.

Bri had that fact and other important info on color-coded cards—red for emergency numbers, orange for house rules, yellow for food, blue for bedtime, green for likes and dislikes. She punched holes in the cards and put them on a binder ring. She had one ring for each kid she babysat.

McCoy called for her right on schedule. Once she'd delivered the water, she flopped down on the couch. She might have to take McCoy to the bathroom once before his parents came home, but otherwise, he should be good. She shot her best friend Lily a text.

craving gumdrops post candy land. brought healthy snacks. Boo to h.s.

Lily instantly texted back.

gdrops are gross cept the black ones. wanna watch The Ep?

Bri thumbed in her answer.

at 13 after.

She pulled up *The Fosters* on Netflix and selected the season two finale, to be known forever as The Ep. The one where Callie and Brandon kissed. When he looked at her like that. When it was so obvious he loved her. So obvious, even if Brandon didn't realize it all the time.

As soon as it was 8:13, she hit the "play" arrow. Bri and Lily had an agreement that they would only watch The Ep together, but that watching it at exactly the same time in different locations counted.

Lily texted as soon as the episode ended.

i want a brandon. love goddess, i implore you, bring me a Brandon

Bri replied right away.

my brandon is david massey

Just typing David's name made Bri's stomach do a little flip-flop. Lily's reply popped up just a second later.

lucky ducky. i don't have a brandon in sight. yet. and now you know i must ask—when are you going to actually speak to the boy?

Good question.

ummmmmm

Lily shot back another text.

he's never going to know how fab you are if you just keep staring from afar. and you won't know if he is truly brandon-y if you never talk to him.

McCoy called for her, preventing another variation of a conversation she and Lily had already had about a thousand times before. Lily didn't think it was possible for Bri to know David was the guy for her just by looking at him while trying not to drool.

Bri quickly typed.

Then she dropped her phone, grabbed the Monster Away spray bottle (the toilet always needed protection on nighttime bathroom runs), and hurried to McCoy's room. *Just because you've never actually talked to someone doesn't mean you can't know what they're like, right?* she thought as she led the boy down the hall. *I mean, I'm in classes with him. I see him. I see how he acts. I've observed him for almost two months. I'm talking close observation. With notes. I so know him.*

Once McCoy was tucked back in, Bri returned to the couch. She flopped down and let her head drop over the edge. She decided to play a few rounds of Candy Crush and grabbed her cell off the coffee table. She'd almost cracked level 303, when she heard a key turning in the lock of the front door.

"Sleeping?" Mr. Rankin asked when he and Mrs. Rankin came into the living room.

"Sleeping," Bri answered. She launched into the McCoy report. Parents always wanted to know what their kids ate, if they went to bed on time, and if they had any meltdowns. Bri always gave them a rundown right away. Tonight she even had a visual aid—a couple of selfies of her and McCoy pretending to be kitties. The Rankins weren't the kind of parents who would mind the ketchup whiskers.

"So cute!" Mrs. Rankin exclaimed. "You have to send me those pics."

"On it," Bri said, thumbs darting over the screen of her phone.

"I love how you always find something fun to do with him," Mrs. Rankin continued. Mr. Rankin nodded in agreement.

"Come on, I'll drive you home," Mrs. Rankin said as Bri slid her phone back in her pocket. She gathered her stuff and headed out to the Nissan with Mrs. Rankin. "Would it be okay if I give your number to a woman who just joined my book group?" Mrs. Rankin asked once they were on the road. "She and her family moved to town at the beginning of the school year, and she hasn't found a babysitter yet."

"Sure. That would be great. Thanks!" Bri answered.

"You just have to promise if we both try to book you for the same day that I get dibs. I found you first," Mrs. Rankin said, playfully waving one finger at Bri.

Bri laughed. "I promise. What's her name?"

"Mrs. Massey."

"Mrs. Massey?" Bri repeated. *Massey. Newish in town. Could it be? COULD IT BE?*

"Do you know how old the kids are?" she asked. *Please say there's one in middle school. Pleeeease,* she silently begged.

"One's in preschool. One's in first or second grade," Mrs. Rankin told her.

For a few magical moments, Bri had thought she had a chance to babysit in David Massey's house. The house in which David Massey lived. Where she would possibly see David Massey, and where, unlike in math and social studies, he'd have to talk to her, because, well, it would be insanely rude not to, and it wasn't like him to be rude. She was sure of that.

But no. Mrs. Rankin hadn't mentioned a kid who could be David. The Masseys she was talking about couldn't be Bri's Masseys. Well, David Massey's Masseys.

"There's also a brother about your age, thirteen or fourteen, I think," Mrs. Rankin added. "He usually watches the kids when needed, but I guess he has after-school commitments sometimes. I don't remember what."

Yes! Yessss! Yesyesyes! Yee-haw! Bingo! Bri couldn't come up with the words to express how perfect/amazing/wonderful this was.

"We're here," Mrs. Rankin said.

Whoops! Bri had been so caught up in her euphoria that she hadn't realized they were in front of her house. "Remember I have dibs on you," Mrs. Rankin said as she paid Bri.

"I will," Bri promised. But it would be hard to pass up a chance to be at the Massey's, where she might see David.

She got out of the car and started up her front walk. She looked over at Lily's house. Her bedroom light was on, and Bri's news should be delivered in person.

She quickly sent her bestie a text.

can I come over for a sec? got news. big news.

Lily answered by flicking the lights once. When they were little, before they were allowed to have cell phones, they'd created a flashing-light code and used it to talk to each other by turning their bedroom lights on and off.

Bri grinned as she dashed across Lily's front lawn. Lily swung the front door open just as Bri was bounding up the porch steps. "What?" Lily exclaimed. "Tell me, tell me!"

"I think your Love Goddess just came through for me!" Bri said breathlessly.

"Why? What happened?" Lily cried.

"Mrs. Rankin just asked me if she could give my number to Mrs. Massey—as in David Massey's mother—because she needs a sitter for David's younger brother and sister. It looks like I'm going to be spending time in David Massey's house!"

"That's . . . that's amazing," Lily answered.

"Has to be your Love Goddess at work, doesn't it?" Bri asked. She wanted to hear her friend say, again, how incredible Bri getting asked to babysit at the Massey's was.

"For sure," Lily answered, shoving her curly blond hair behind her ears. "And it's so unfair. You don't even believe in the Love Goddess, and you get her acting on your behalf before I do." She gave an exaggerated pout, but it quickly turned into a smile.

"I'm sure she hasn't forgotten about you, Lils. It's just that it will take a while to find a boy awesome enough for awesome you," Bri said. She glanced over at her house. "I should get home."

"Not before we dance, you don't." Lily pulled her phone out of her pocket. As always, a pair of ear buds was attached. She put one of the buds into her ear and handed the other one to Bri. A few seconds later, pop music was blasting in Bri's ear, and she and Lily were doing the happy dance they'd invented in fourth grade to celebrate Lily's braces coming off.

Bri tilted her head back and shouted up to the stars. "Thank you, Love Goddess!" It turned out she really did exist after all! And she was on the job, bringing David Massey and Bri together!

When you're babysitting, wear shoes you can run in and clothes you don't mind getting dirty, and avoid dangly earrings. (Babies like to pull on them—ouch!)

Chapter 2

As soon as the last bell rang on Wednesday, Bri bolted to her locker. She was so impatient to get it open that she messed up the combination—twice. She sucked in a long breath and carefully dialed in the combination again. When she pulled on the lock, it opened with a soft, satisfying click.

Bri couldn't believe that the school made kids leave their phones in their lockers except at lunch. Didn't they understand that some situations were urgent? What if Mrs. Massey had called to ask Bri to babysit and then called a different sitter because Bri didn't answer the phone?

She snatched up the phone and checked for texts and then for missed calls and then for texts again, just to be sure. Finally, she checked for missed calls again, because maybe she'd looked too fast the first time.

No. Nope. Nothing. Nothing from anyone. Big nothing from Mrs. Massey.

Bri made sure the phone wasn't on vibrate-only and checked that the volume was still as high as it would go. She kept it in her hand instead of putting it in her pocket. She wanted to be prepared to answer it fast—first-ring fast.

"No call," Lily said as she came over, her back-pack slung over one shoulder.

"It's that obvious?" Bri asked.

"To me, it is," Lily answered. "You'd be all . . ." She made jazz hands by her face while grinning wide enough to show every tooth. ". . . if you'd heard from her." Bri had made Lily promise not to use Mrs. Massey's name at school. She didn't want anyone overhearing and maybe saying something to David. That would be humiliating.

"Your Love Goddess is heartless," Bri complained. "It's been four and a half days since I told

Mrs. Raskin she could give *her* the number. Four and a half very quiet days."

"You'll get the call," Lily assured her. "As soon as she actually needs a sitter. You know Mrs. Raskin would rave about you. There's no reason she would call anyone else."

Bri jerked her phone up in front of her face but then let her hand drop back to her side. "I thought I felt it vibrate," she said. Then she jerked her hand back up so she could check that the volume was still all the way up.

"Be patient," Lily told her. "When it's meant to happen, it will happen."

Bri let out a growl of frustration. She and Lily were so different. Bri wasn't the kind of person who could calmly wait for something to happen. She was the kind of person who made things happen herself.

But she couldn't make the phone ring.

At 6:12 that night, Bri lay on her bed staring at her phone. Her superb, magnificent, gorgeous phone. She gave it a kiss and then used the hem of her T-shirt to wipe off the pale pink Born With It lipgloss the kiss had left behind. She texted Lily.

it!!!!! happened!!!! need you immediately!!!!

Lily must have run all the way from her house, because the doorbell rang less than a minute later. "Tell her to come up," Bri yelled down to her mom. "Please," she added.

"I can't help it. I'm saying it—I told you so," Lily said as she walked into Bri's bedroom.

"Yeah, yeah, yeah! You were right," Bri said. She flung open both doors of her closet. Inside, all of her clothes were arranged by color so it was kind of like looking at a rainbow. "Now what am I going to wear? It has to be babysitter-appropriate. Casual and nothing I'd worry about getting stains on. And not too tight or anything. But also, and much more importantly, it has to be cute—extremely cute."

"Got it. How much time do we have? When do you have to be there?" Lily asked, already flicking through hangers.

"Five-thirty on Friday," Bri answered. She dropped to her knees. "Shoes are important. Maybe my turquoise Chucks. Chucks say cool and fun and not trying too hard, don't you think?"

When Lily didn't answer, Bri looked up. Lily was staring at her. "Did you say Friday?" she finally asked.

"Yeah, Friday. This Friday. So there's not much time." Bri returned to pawing through her shoes.

"You do realize it's Wednesday," Lily said.

"I might need to wash something. Or buy something!" Bri answered, speaking so fast her words were in danger of crashing into each other. "Except I can't, because I'm babysitting tomorrow night. So it has to be something I already have."

"You have lots of cute stuff," Lily answered. She had a lot of experience decoding Bri's super-fast speech. "How about your 'Strange Is Just

More Interesting' T-shirt? It's the perfect degree of worn."

"*Hmm*." Bri pulled the shirt out of the closet and studied it. "I wonder if David would think it's funny. I know he has a good sense of humor. I hear him laughing with his friends. I just don't know if he'd think the 'Strange' tee is too strange. He wears blue a lot. Maybe I should wear something blue. It might be his favorite color."

Lily turned away from the closet and flopped down on Bri's bed. "I don't think you need to strategize so much. He's not going to like you or not like you because you're wearing his favorite—possibly his favorite—color. He's going to like you because you two click. It's not something you can plan."

"Everything's better with a plan," Bri answered.

"If you're writing a report or something," Lily agreed. "But I don't think you can really come up with a plan to make somebody like you."

Bri snorted. "Of course you can. And it starts with the right outfit. Maybe this?" She held out an orange sweatshirt with a big white heart in the center. Before Lily could answer, Bri put it back in its place.

"Don't freak, but you know David might not even be there, right?" Lily asked. "I'm not trying to be all negative. I just want you to be prepared. You told me Mrs. Rankin said he usually stays with the younger kids unless he's doing something. Which kind of means he's probably doing something Friday night."

"But his mom told me that she and her husband were going to be out until about eleven. I doubt David's going to get home from whatever he's doing later than that," Bri answered. "It will be perfect. The kids will be in bed, so I won't have to worry about them when I'm talking to David."

"Yeah, he should be home at least a little of the time," Lily agreed. "And even though you'd probably be able to leave once he's back, you'd still get a chance to hang with him a little."

Bri's heart started beating a little faster. She wanted to talk to David, but it was a little scary to think about.

"Call your mom and ask if you can stay for dinner," Bri said. "Once we figure out what I should wear, we need to come up with some good topics of conversation. "I'm pretty sure he said he was into that game Terraria."

"Wait. You talked to him? More than saying hi?" Lily sat up. "That's great! How could you not tell me that?"

"He wasn't actually talking to me," Bri admitted. "He was talking to Chris Neemy. I just happened to hear."

"You're not stalking him, are you?" Lily exclaimed.

"Of course not," Bri said. "I just *happened* to be right behind him and Chris when we were leaving math class."

"Just happened. Uh-huh. Of course." Lily smiled as she shook her head at Bri.

"Okay, I almost knocked over McKenzie so I'd happen to be right behind him," Bri admitted with a smile. "But I only did it because eavesdropping on David will help me come up with better topics of conversation for when we're together at his house."

"Okay, so he likes Terraria. What else have you figured out, Nancy Drew?"

"He likes blue. And he's good at math, but I'm not sure that would make a good conversation," Bri said. What if she said the wrong thing? What if she messed up?

She wouldn't. She couldn't. Because she'd have a plan! She'd figure out everything she possibly could, and she'd be fine. No, she'd be great!

When you're babysitting, respect the family's privacy. Don't go into rooms there's no reason for you to be in.

Chapter 3

Bri studied herself in the mirror. Did her ears stick out too much? Was the headband a bad decision? She wore headbands all the time, and she'd never noticed an ear issue. But now . . .

She pressed her fingertips against the tops of her ears. She was being crazy, wasn't she? She took a step closer to the mirror, turning her head from side to side.

Whirling around, she grabbed her cell off her night stand. Lily would tell her the truth.

need complete honesty. are my ears sticky-outy?

Lily responded right away:

i fear you are losing it. my friend

Bri's thumbs flew over her cell.

just tell me. tell me. hair pulled back with headband or not.

headband is good. no headband is good. ears not sticky-outy. my grandmother says you're a very pretty girl. and we know she doesn't bother being polite ever.

Bri let out a long sigh.

thx. ttyl.

She put on her favorite fitted denim jacket. "Mom, I'm ready to go," she called. She was half-way down the stairs when she realized she'd forgotten to put index cards in her purse. She always put the info parents gave her on index cards.

She hurried to her desk and got cards in each of the five colors she used to organize the facts about the kids she sat for. She started downstairs again. This time she reached the front hall before she realized she'd forgotten something else. "One sec," she told her mom, who was waiting for her, car keys in hand.

Bri was losing it. First she forgot the index cards; now she'd forgotten her Mary Poppins bag.

If she didn't watch out, she'd blow this babysitting job and never get asked to sit for the Masseys again.

She rushed back to her room, picked up the Poppins bag from her bed, and closed her eyes for a moment. "Calm down," she whispered. "*Calmdowncalmdowncalmdown.*" Saying this actually made her feel a little more nervous.

Her cell beeped. Bri decided she had time to check it. A text from Lily.

> if david doesn't think you're great, he's crazy, and you don't want a crazy boy. if it turns out he's kookoo i know the Love Goddess will come through with somebody better.

Bri thought about how cute David was when he laughed and how serious he always looked when he was doing a math problem at the board. She thought about how he always jerked his head back to get his shaggy, sandy-brown hair off his face and how he picked her pencil up for her that time she dropped it. She sent a reply to Lily.

he's perfect. but thanks.

good luck!!!

Bri glanced in the mirror one last time. *You don't need luck,* she told herself. She'd achieved maximum cuteness combined with casualness. She and Lily had come up with a list of conversation starters and ways to keep the conversation going once it was started. *You don't need luck, because you have a plan.*

"Bedtime Piper—7:30. Bedtime Elijah—8:30," Bri wrote on a blue index card. She sat at the Massey's kitchen table with Mrs. Massey. She could hear some kid noises from the back of the house, but she hadn't been introduced to Elijah and Piper yet. Was David back there with the little kids? Or had he left already? She thought she'd heard a lower voice, but that could be Mr. Massey.

Bri suddenly realized Mrs. Massey was looking at her, like she was waiting for something.

Something like Bri's next question! "Is it okay for them to look at books or play with toys after they're in bed?" she asked. "Or is it lights out right away?"

She wrote down Mrs. Massey's response. "What about special blankets or stuffed animals?"

After answering, Mrs. Massey said, "You're really thorough. I appreciate that. I shouldn't be surprised. Mrs. Rankin said you were wonderful." She stood up. "I'll go get the kids." She paused as she headed toward the kitchen door. "I put all the important numbers on the fridge. My cell. My husband's cell. Fire. Doctor. Poison control. Emergency room. Baileys—that's the neighbors next door. Pizza delivery."

Yikes! How could Bri have forgotten to ask for emergency numbers? Usually the first thing she did was fill out the red card with all that info. Making sure to get those numbers was one of the first things they'd taught at the Red Cross babysitting class she'd taken.

As soon as Mrs. Massey left the kitchen, Bri went to the fridge and copied down the numbers onto a red index card. Her stomach did a flip when she heard footsteps coming in her direction. A moment later, the kitchen door swung open and Mrs. Massey came in, followed by a boy about seven years old, a girl about four, and a man whom Bri assumed was Mr. Massey.

No David.

"This is Elijah and Piper," Mrs. Massey told Bri. "And my husband, Mark."

She turned to the kids. "This is Bri, the babysitter who will be staying with you. Be good for her, okay?"

Elijah muttered an "okay." Piper just pressed her face into her mother's leg. "She's a little shy," Mrs. Massey whispered. Bri nodded.

"You have our numbers if you need them, right?" Mr. Massey asked.

"Of course she has the numbers," Mrs. Massey answered with a smile.

Why weren't either of them saying anything about David? If he were at home right now, they'd definitely say something. But weren't they even going to mention that he'd be coming home at some point? Weren't they going to tell her if she should leave or stay once he was back?

She dragged her attention back to Elijah and Piper as their parents said good-bye. That was a tricky time for a lot of kids. As much as they liked their babysitter, a lot of them didn't want their parents to go. The first time was usually the worst, unless the kids were neighbors and already knew Bri.

"Don't you have an older son too?" Bri asked just as Mr. Massey was closing the door behind them. "Will he take over if he gets home first?"

He swung the door wide. "He's staying over at a friend's tonight, so you're on your own until we get back."

"No worries. We'll have lots of fun," Bri told him, trying to keep any trace of disappointment out of her voice. There wasn't going to be any time alone with David after the kids were asleep. She wasn't even going to get a glimpse of him. It was truly unfair of Lily's Love Goddess, getting Bri's hopes up only to stomp on them.

Elijah and Piper didn't look happy when their parents said good-bye again and shut the door, but neither got close to a meltdown. "Mom said you're supposed to make us chicken nuggets and tater tots for dinner," Elijah informed Bri.

Clearly, he was one of those kids who wanted to be boss. At least he'd told her exactly the same thing his mom had—except he'd left out the broccoli—instead of trying to con her.

"I will," Bri assured him. "I'll pop them in the oven in about a half an hour." That way they'd be ready at six-thirty when Mrs. Massey said they usually ate dinner.

"I heard chicken nuggets are one of your favorites," she said to Piper. The little girl just stared at Bri with her big blue eyes.

The same color as David's, Bri realized, *like a summer sky.*

She suddenly felt a little more cheerful. She was still in David's house, with David's brother and sister. She bet she could learn a ton of stuff about David—stuff that she could use when she actually did get a chance to talk to him!

"Does your big brother like chicken nuggets too?" Bri asked, glancing from Piper to Elijah. She had to admit, though, it was a pretty dumb question. It's not like she and David were going to bond while chatting about frozen food products.

Piper continued to stare at her without speaking. "I get to stay up however long I want," Elijah informed her, ignoring her question.

Ah. So there wouldn't just be bossing. There would also be some testing of the new babysitter, Bri thought.

No problem. She'd dealt with this before. Keeping her tone casual and a little apologetic, Bri said, "Oh, your mom said eight-thirty. I must have gotten it wrong. Sorry. Let me just call her to check." She reached for her phone.

"Never mind. Eight-thirty is okay," Elijah muttered.

"Great! So what should we do until dinner? Are there any games you like to play? What do you play with your big brother?" Bri asked. Okay, that was two David questions in less than two minutes. She needed to calm down. But at least the second question might give her something she could use to talk to David.

She should have brainstormed some ways to gather information from the kids without being obvious about it. She didn't want one of them telling David that their babysitter kept asking questions about him.

"I'll just play my Game Boy." Elijah started for the kitchen door.

Mrs. Massey had said to limit his screen time to an hour. Bri didn't want to start off the night with a battle. It was time to hit the Poppins bag.

"I know something great we can do!" she exclaimed. She had a box of cornstarch in the bag. All you had to do was add some water and voila—you got this weird gunk that could be squishy or hard. It could even bounce depending on the ratio of cornstarch to water. It was definitely something a four-year-old and a seven-year-old would love.

"What?" Piper asked softly. It was the first word she'd spoken since her parents left.

"We're going to . . ." Bri's words trailed off as she realized that the Poppins bag wasn't on the table with her purse. She'd left it in the car! She couldn't believe she'd forgotten it twice in one night! She'd clearly been using most of her brain to daydream about David.

"We're going to play hide-and-seek!" It was the first thing that came into her mind. But it should work. The game was a classic, and a four-year-old and seven-year-old could definitely play it together. "I'll be It!" Bri rushed on, not leaving time for protests. She covered her eyes with both hands and began to count. She smiled as she heard footsteps rushing away from her.

Hide-and-seek is actually perfect for intel gathering, Bri realized as she continued counting. David wasn't home. She could take a little peek in his room. That wasn't really snooping. One of the kids might have decided to hide in there. It would be completely normal for her to go in.

"Ready or not, here I come!" Bri called, her heart pitter-pattering with anticipation.

Who knew what she'd discover in David's room? Maybe she could get a look at his Spotify playlist. Although it's not like the kids would be hiding inside his laptop. But what if David loved Sam Smith as much as she did? Maybe he'd come play at the Varsity, and the two of them could go. She'd wear her—

Bri realized she was still standing in the middle of the kitchen. Her daydreaming brain was out of control!

She headed into the living room. "I wonder where Elijah and Piper could be hiding," she said. Kids always loved it when they thought you were having a hard time finding them. Actually, as soon as she'd walked into the room, Bri had seen Piper's shoes sticking out from under the living room curtains.

Bri made a big show of looking around from floor to ceiling as she crossed the room. Piper started to giggle, but Bri pretended she didn't notice. "They're not in here, that's for sure." The giggling got louder as she started down the hall.

Piper sounded like she was having fun. That made Bri feel a little less guilty. She wasn't doing anything wrong. She was playing a game with the kids she was sitting for, which is what she always did when she babysat. Getting the scoop on David was just a bonus.

Slowly, Bri opened the first door in the hallway—bathroom. She loudly opened and shut the cupboards under the sink and whipped back the shower curtain around the tub. Elijah reared up with a dinosaur roar.

Dang it! She hadn't realized he was in there. If she had, she wouldn't have opened the curtain. She'd have checked out David's room first.

"Got you!" Bri exclaimed. "Now I just have to find Piper. She's a really good hider."

Bri stepped back into the hall, Elijah on her heels. She wasn't going to be able to snoop around in David's room with him trailing her. She'd have to wait for the next round.

"She always hides behind the curtains in the living room," Elijah told Bri as she opened the next door down the hallway. The canopy bed crammed with stuffed animals told her it was Piper's room.

"I already checked the living room, and I didn't see her," Bri said loudly enough that Piper would be able to hear her. A giggle came in response.

"I told you," Elijah said. "Come on." He turned around and started for the living room. Bri had to go with him. As soon as they went into the room, he triumphantly pointed at the Piper feet.

Bri tiptoed over with exaggerated motions and tickled the lump behind the curtain. "Do you have a cat?" she asked Elijah. "It feels like there's a big kitty on the windowsill."

"It's me!" Piper exclaimed, popping out from behind the curtains.

"And I was sure it was a cat!" Bri told her. She looked over at Elijah. "I found you first. That means you're It this time."

Elijah immediately covered his eyes and started counting. Piper pulled back the curtains, getting ready to hide in the same spot.

Bri put her finger to her lips, slipped off Piper's shoes, and positioned them with the toes peeping out from under the curtain. Then she took Piper by the hand and helped the excited little girl hide in the narrow broom closet next to the fridge. Maybe that would keep Elijah busy long enough for Bri to get her snoop on.

Bri found David's room in just a few moments. She slipped inside. The first thing she noticed was that David was kind of a slob. A pile of clothes had been hurled into one corner, and a plate and a glass sat on the floor next to the bed. But that didn't matter to Bri. Lily wasn't exactly Ms. Clean, and she and Bri still managed to be best friends.

"Ready or not, here I come!" she heard Elijah shout. She might not have much more time. She scurried to David's desk. She touched the lid of his laptop, but couldn't bring herself to open it. There was snooping, and then there was SNOOPING. She'd stick to peeking at stuff that was out in the open.

Math homework.

English homework.

And—yes! *Yesyesyes*! Bingo and woo-hoo!

David had made a list of his favorite stuff. An actual list! It actually said, "FAVORITES" at the top of it.

She whipped out her phone and took a picture of it. Then she took another just in case the first one was blurry.

With this list, she could make herself into the kind of girl David would be absolutely unable to resist!

Make simple snacks with the kids, like mini pizzas using bagels as crusts. But be sure to ask parents about food allergies before serving anything.

Chapter 4

"Weekend? Weekend? Weekend? Weekend?" Megan asked as soon everyone was seated at the usual lunch table on Monday morning. "Everyone" was Megan, Bri, Lily, Abby, and Sophia.

"Bri has to go first," Lily said. "Unless one of you signed up for that one-way Mars mission, she has the most to tell."

"*Ooooh,*" Abby, Megan, and Sophia cried in unison. They burst out in giggles.

Bri wished Lily hadn't said that. It wasn't that Bri didn't plan to tell the other three girls about the list of David's favorite stuff. Just not yet. She'd planned on telling them later. Much later. After she and David had started hanging out or at least talking to each other sometimes, telling them about her snooping and the list she'd found would just be a funny story. "Come on, tell us," Sophia said when Bri hesitated.

"You know how I told you David Massey's mom might ask me to babysit for his younger brother and sister?" Bri asked.

"Yeah. And?" Abby leaned toward her.

"And she called me. And I babysat over there on Friday night," Bri answered.

"Did you see him? What did he say? What did you say?" Megan exclaimed. Megan never asked just one question at a time.

"No, so nothing and nothing," Bri said.

"Still, you might get asked again, and then you might get to talk to him," Sophia said. Sophia was always encouraging.

Lily usually encouraged her too, but she'd acted more than a little judgmental when Bri told her how she planned to use the list she found in David's room to turn herself into his ideal, perfect girl.

Megan looked back and forth between Lily and Bri. "That's not the whole story though, am I right? What's going on? Did something happen when you were over at his house?"

"I was playing hide-and-seek, and I ended up hiding in David's room," Bri admitted. She didn't say that she'd gone in there on purpose to gather intel, and Lily didn't jump in and tell everyone that was what really happened. "I saw this list of his favorite stuff on his desk."

"That's so great!" Abby cried. "Now you'll have a ton of things you can talk to him about. He'll think you're so cool because you'll like all the stuff he likes."

"Yes!" Bri cried, slapping her hand on the table. "See? Abby gets it," she told Lily.

"But she hasn't heard what was on the list," Lily said. "You guys, Bri doesn't like anything on the list. Not one thing. I just think it's . . . it doesn't make sense to twist yourself into this whole other person just to get somebody to like you."

She shot Bri an apologetic look. "I mean, Bri's fab already," Lily added.

"Extremely fab," Sophia agreed.

"It's not like I hate the stuff on this list, though," Bri said. "I just don't know much about most of the things. They might actually turn out to be my favorites too, once I try them."

"So what's on the list?" Abby asked, leaning in even closer—so close she was in danger of getting spaghetti sauce from Bri's plate on her shirt.

Bri pulled the pic of the list up on her phone, even though she'd had it memorized before she fell asleep on Friday night. "Anime, the show *MasterChef Junior*, that folk band Just Us Folks, marathons, horror movies—"

"Horror movies?" Sophia interrupted. "Bri, you won't even go on the Lost Dutchman Mine Ride at Fun Village because it's too spooky. How are you going to watch a horror movie?"

"I went on it once," Bri protested. "And I wasn't scared. I just didn't like how those miner ghosts pop out at you. Plus, the howling hurt my ears."

"Maybe you could skip the horror movie part of the list. It's not really you," Sophia suggested.

Lily nodded vigorously but didn't say anything. Bri gave her a little frown. "Lily thinks there's no way David and I would possibly have any fun together because we're too different."

"I didn't say that," Lily said. "I know people who like different things can like each other. Which is why I don't think you have to pretend to like everything David likes if you want him to like you."

"Yeah, I like you, and I hate those stupid comedies you love," Sophia told Bri.

"Look, all I want is to have a few things to talk to David about, okay?" She turned to Abby. "If you had inside info on Christopher Lakshmin, you'd use it to get him to notice you, wouldn't you? How could you ignore that?"

"Christopher Lakshmin. Swoon. Yes," Abby answered. Abby was crushing on Christopher almost as hard as Bri was crushing on David. Maybe Lily just didn't get it because she wasn't crushing on anybody. She was still waiting for the Love Goddess to bring the right boy to her.

Megan had no interest in having a boyfriend right now. She had three sisters, and one of them was always in some kind of boy-induced melt-down. Megan didn't want the drama.

And Sophia only crushed on actors and musicians, not guys that she'd actually have to talk to.

Why wouldn't Lily accept that sometimes even the Love Goddess might need an assist? Maybe the L.G. had gotten Bri into David's house but expected Bri to take it from there.

"So Abby's on my side," Bri said, reaching across the table to give Abby a high five.

"Wait. I'm not *not* on your side," Lily protested.

"Really?" Bri asked. It had seemed like her best friend didn't support her, and that was a terrible feeling. "So you'll help me with the list?"

"Of course I'll help you. I just think you should

trust the Love Goddess more. There's somebody out there who will be perfect for the actual you." Lily smiled at Bri. "And who knows. Maybe it's David. If it is, no worries. You won't have to change anything."

Bri gave a sigh. "Lils, why won't you just accept that—"

"I'll help too," Sophie jumped in.

"I'm in," Abby said.

"Like I have anything better to do," Megan joked. "So what do you need us to do? What's the plan? When do we start?"

"We start now," Bri answered. This was great! With her friends behind her, she'd be an expert in anime, horror movies, long-distance running, and all of David's other favorite stuff in no time!

"Mrs. Massey called me last night. I'm officially babysitting for the Masseys every Wednesday and Friday night for six weeks, starting this

Friday," Bri announced two days later, when she and her friends were all gathered at their usual lunch table again. "There should definitely be some David overlap. He has basketball practice on Wednesday night, but usually gets home by eight-thirty. I can go when he gets home, but that doesn't mean I have to leave if, for instance, we start talking."

"What about on Friday nights?" Megan asked. "Will he ever be home? He was over at a friend's the last time, right?"

"Sometimes he has games, and sometimes he has plans with his friends. They wanted to sign me up for all six Fridays, so they'd be sure to have a sitter. They know Fridays are popular nights for parents to go out. Some Friday nights he might be home at least part or maybe all of the time I'll be there, but I'll be in charge of the kids." Bri smiled at Lily. "The Cash Goddess might be helping me out too. Mrs. Rankin just booked me for two Sunday nights!"

Bri opened her backpack and started pulling out cookbooks and passing them around the table. For once, she was happy David didn't have the same lunch period she did. This way, she could use the time to prep with her friends. "I decided to start with the *MasterChef Junior* part of the list," she said. "On Friday, I'm going to make the kids dinner—actual dinner—not just throw some frozen chicken nuggets in the oven. I told Mrs. Massey I wanted cooking practice, and she said I could. So now we have to find some recipes that will show off my *MasterChef Junior* skills."

"Which you do not yet have," Abby teased with a smile.

"She said it, not me," Lily said, holding up both hands. "You should make something the kids might actually want to eat. So nothing too weird."

"So what do they like? Do you know? Are they super picky?" Megan asked. "I had a cousin who would only eat peanut-butter-and-potato-chip sandwiches. That's all he ate for an entire year.

Even for breakfast. That's so weird, isn't it? Weird and kind of disgusting, right? Do you think it qualifies as some sort of illness?"

Bri ignored the questions about Megan's cousin's eating habits. She wanted to keep this conversation on track. "I was thinking chicken. I know the kids like chicken nuggets, so I thought if I just did a fancier version, that would work. So let's focus on the chicken sections," Bri said, doing an imitation of their social studies teacher's prissy attitude.

"I can't look at chicken," Sophie said with a grimace.

"Oh, right."

Sophie was a vegetarian. She couldn't stand the idea of eating anything that once had a face, even if that face had a beak.

"I need a dessert too. Why don't you work on that, Sophie?" Bri suggested. "It should be something unique. I think the kids would be up for trying any kind of dessert, so go wild. Think something that would make Chef Ramsey—and, more importantly, David—say wowza."

"Chef Ramsey has never uttered the word *wowza*," Abby said. "I remember he called one dessert a 'banana-flavored cloud', but that's as good as it gets."

"Do you actually memorize Chef Ramsay quotes?" Bri asked.

"I don't try. They just kind of worm into my brain. And it's not just Chef Ramsay—it's all TV judges," Abby answered.

"I just found some actual *MasterChef Junior* recipes," Lily announced, waving her phone. "And there's one for five-spice chicken wings!"

"Perfect!" Bri grinned. Even though Lily didn't totally agree with Bri's plan to make David like her, Lils was doing all she could to help.

Lily frowned. "Except that for the dipping sauce you need Sriracha chili sauce and a tool called a nitrous oxide foamer. I don't know what either of those is."

Bri looked at Abby. Abby shrugged. "I watch for the drama, not the actual cooking."

"Let's keep looking," Lily suggested. "We can find something easier."

"But I think Lily's idea of doing an recipe from the show is great. It said *MasterChef Junior* on the list, so let's stick with the *MasterChef* recipe," Bri answered. "Maybe I could substitute salsa for the part of the recipe that uses Sriracha chili sauce. Salsa is sort of like chili sauce."

"Definitely," Sophie said.

"I think it's so great you're doing this," Abby added. "You might inspire me to talk to Christopher. Or at least say hi."

"Maybe I'll write Jacob Latimer a letter. I can tell him how awesome I thought he was in *Maze Runner*," Sophia said.

"And how much you love his big brown eyes," Abby joked.

"Honey mustard is really good on wings," Megan said. She'd returned her attention Bri's cooking. "Could you use that? Or bleu cheese dressing? Or ranch dressing?" Megan asked.

"Any of those would be a good substitution," Lily said.

Bri shook her head. "Too ordinary. To get David's attention, it has to be special. I have tonight and tomorrow night to figure out how to make everything."

"But what if David doesn't come home again? What if he has plans? What if he's staying over at a friend's the way he did last time?" Megan asked.

She was right. That could happen. It had happened the last time. What if David liked having someone else look after his brother and sister once in a while? What if he never came home when she was there?

Panic jolted through Bri for a few seconds, but she quickly realized there was a solution. "Leftovers!" she cried. "If he's not home, I'll leave leftovers. So no matter what happens, David will find out I'm a gourmet cook!"

Sometimes it's impossible to stop a tantrum from happening. Stay calm. After the tantrum ends, help the child deal with the upsetting feelings by talking them through.

Chapter 5

"My mom said I don't have to eat what you make if I don't like it. She said if I don't like it, you have to make me peanut butter and jelly," Elijah informed Bri on Friday night as Bri unpacked groceries onto the Massey's kitchen counter. She'd spent more on the food than she'd make babysitting tonight, but it was okay. She had some cash saved up.

And Project David, as she'd started calling it, was worth it.

"I will absolutely make you peanut butter and jelly if that's what you want," Bri promised him. "You too, Piper. But I think the dinner I'm making is going to be yummy. It's chicken wings. You like those, right?"

"Like from Domino's?" Elijah asked.

"Yeah! Like from Domino's!" Bri told him, pumping as much enthusiasm into her voice as possible. If you acted excited about something, kids would usually get excited about it too. And she was excited about making the wings. It's just that the excitement was mixed with nervousness.

"Domino's?" Piper cried. "Yay, pizza!"

Uh-oh, Bri thought. She knelt down in front of Piper. "We're going to have chicken wings. I'm going to make them, and you can be my helper. "

"Okay," Piper said, the pizza forgotten.

Bri looked at Elijah. "You can help too."

"I'll play Game Boy," he answered. The console was already sitting on the kitchen table.

"All right, but that will count as part of your screentime," Bri said. He was allowed an hour, and she should be done cooking by then. Elijah nodded, eyes already locked on his game.

"What do I do?" Piper asked.

Bri sucked in a deep breath and brought up the recipe on her cell. She had the chicken soaking in plastic baggies filled with marinade. Her dad had helped her mix it up the night before. He liked to barbeque and was good with marinades.

"First we're going to do some mixing," Bri answered. Mrs. Massey had given her a quick tour of the kitchen, so Bri knew where to find the sauce pans. She got one out and put it on the kitchen table. "I'm going to measure out ingredients and you're going to stir them up." She handed Piper a wooden spoon.

"Just do what the recipe says. You'll be fine," she murmured to herself. She measured out water and molasses into a small saucepan. "Your turn," she told Piper. The little girl's forehead furrowed in concentration as she began to stir.

"Good job!" Bri told her and slapped her a high-five. She liked having a helper. It made her feel more confident to tell Piper each step. "The next thing we do is pour the marinade in." She opened one of the Ziploc bags and started to pour the liquid into the sauce pan, making sure not to let the wings fall out.

"You're putting chicken juice in there?" Elijah sounded horrified.

"It's not chicken juice," Bri said. "It's just some spices and oil I was soaking the wings in. Chicken wings always have spices on them."

"I'm having peanut butter and jelly," Elijah said.

"No problem at all," Bri answered. David would understand that little kids didn't always like to try new food.

Bri turned on the oven so it would be ready for the wings, lit a burner, and placed the saucepan on it. "Now I'm just going to stir this for a—"

"No!" Piper shouted. "I get to stir!"

"You stirred. And you did a fantastic job," Bri told her. "But now I have to put the pan on the stove and you can't stir—"

Piper interrupted again. "I get to stir!"

A lecture on the dangers of a hot stove wasn't going to work. Bri needed to distract Piper—and fast. But tonight she was prepared. She'd remembered the Poppins bag!

"I have something even more fun for you to do," She told Piper. She grabbed the bag and pulled out a sticker book. "Look! Princess stickers! Who's your fave? Ariel? Belle? Cinderella?"

Piper's lip was quivering. Her eyes were bright with tears that were about to spill down her cheeks. "You said I get to stir."

Yikes. Usually little girls couldn't resist the Disney princesses. "Or I could do your hair like Elsa or Anna," Bri offered. "I have some sparkly hair clips." She groped in the bag and pulled out a couple of glittery blue barrettes. "Do you want one braid or two braids, or maybe a crown of braids on top of your head?" She shot a glance at the saucepan. She needed to start stirring, but if she did, Piper would lose it.

"I stir!" Piper lurched toward the stove, spoon in hand.

Bri caught her by the waist and pulled her back. "You're fast as a bunny, aren't you?" she asked, tickling Piper's sides.

Piper didn't giggle. She howled.

"You made Piper cry!" Elijah accused. "I'm telling."

Bri quickly took out the bubble solution and blower. Still holding Piper, she sank down on the kitchen floor. She began blowing bubbles as fast as she could, but she knew it was too late. Piper's body was heaving with sobs. Bri was going to have to let her cry it out.

"She'll be okay," Bri told Elijah. "She's upset because I told her she could stir and then I told her she couldn't."

"That was dumb," Elijah said.

"Yeah, yeah, it was," Bri agreed.

When Piper's crying downgraded to sniffles, Bri decided she could try talking to her. "I know you're mad because I wouldn't let you stir once the pan was on the stove. But the stove is hot, and I don't want you to get hurt. You know what, though? I have something else you can stir." Bri dampened a paper towel and wiped the tears away. She couldn't believe she hadn't thought of giving Piper another stirring job right away.

Usually, she would have. She was just so focused on the recipe. She wanted the wings and everything else to be perfect.

"Okay," Piper said. Her face was red and tear-streaked. Poor girl.

Bri got out another pan and put in water and lime juice. "Stir this for the rice. But when it's time for it to go on the stove, it's my turn. Deal?"

"Okay," Piper said again. Bri didn't have a chance to wash the molasses and marinade off Piper's spoon before she started stirring. *Well, the rice is going to be on the same plate as the wings,* she thought. *It probably doesn't matter.*

Bri got another spoon for herself and hurried over to the stove. The sauce was bubbling, but that was okay. She hoped. The recipe said to cook it until it was syrupy. She gave it a stir. It was a little hard getting the spoon through it. But it wasn't too thick to be called syrupy. She hoped. She turned off the heat, and put the wings in the oven, Piper still busily stirring the water and lime juice.

"Excellent job," Bri told her. "Now I'm going to put some rice in there and cover it up." She picked up the package of rice.

"Why is it black?" Elijah sounded disgusted.

"Some rice is black," Bri told him.

"It looks gross," Elijah told her.

"It has a nice nutty flavor." She'd read that online and had been planning to toss it into conversation with David if he came home before she left. It sounded like something someone on *MasterChef Junior* would say.

She put the rice in the saucepan and added some spices.

"I'm eating peanut butter," he added.

Bri had the urge to scream, "I know you're eating peanut butter! You've already told me a billion times." But babysitters did not scream, so she just smiled. "I like peanut butter too. But it can be fun to try new things."

Elijah just grunted in response.

Bri set the sauce pan of rice on the stove. *Uh-oh. I forgot to rinse the rice first,* she thought. That was one of the recipe instructions. But the rice was in water, so it would get clean, anyway. She hoped.

She put the lid on the pan. "All right, Miss Piper, what shall we do while dinner cooks?"

Piper wanted a piggyback ride, so Bri carried her around the house until it was time to put the sauce on the chicken. She was supposed to coat the wings, but the sauce was too thick, so she just smushed some clumps of it on with the spoon and put the baking sheet back in the oven.

She turned her attention back to the rice. Elijah was right. It looked gross. Goopy and sludgy and a weird purple-black color, like eggplant. She hated eggplant. But it would have a mild nutty flavor. She hoped.

Piper tugged at the hem of Bri's T-shirt. Bri realized it had a clump of the wing sauce on it. She tried to brush it off, and it left a long reddish-brown streak. Not the casual-but-extremely-cute look she'd been going for. Well, David would understand that cooks got messy. She hoped.

Piper tugged on the shirt again. "More!"

Bri knelt down, let Piper climb aboard, and started another lap around the house. She stopped at Piper's bedroom so Piper could introduce her to all her stuffed animals. The little girl had clearly forgotten all about the Stirring Incident.

"This one is Bun-Bun," Piper explained, holding a stuffed rabbit that looked a lot like the other two she'd already showed Bri. But Bri knew it was important to learn all the animals' names. Okay, Bun-Bun was missing an eye. Bun-Bun equals blind. Floppsy had the longest fur. So Floppsy equals furry. And Mr. Peter equals . . . Mr. Peter wasn't blind or furry. Mr. Peter equals perfect?

Piper unearthed another rabbit from the pile of toys on her bed. How many bunnies did she have? Bri wondered. She was going to have to write up an index card to keep all their names straight. "This one is—" Piper began.

"Something's burning!" Elijah shouted. Bri raced to the kitchen. The smoke alarm began to blare before she could reach the stove.

Beep-beep-beep.

Bri grabbed a potholder and took the lid off the rice. It still looked gross, but it wasn't burning. She opened the oven door. Several of the sauce clumps were smoking. *Stay calm,* she ordered herself. She shut the oven and turned it off. Just to be safe, she turned off the burner too. Then she opened all the kitchen windows.

Beep-beep-beep.

The smoke alarm continued to blast. Piper had her hands over her ears, and Elijah looked freaked. "It's okay," said Bri. "I think the sauce I put on the chicken got too hot and started to smoke. There's no fire. Everything's fine."

She grabbed a dishtowel and started waving it at the smoke detector like her mom always did, but it wasn't helping. Maybe she wasn't getting the towel high enough. She grabbed one of the kitchen chairs and dragged it underneath the smoke detector. She frantically waved the towel.

Beep-beep-beep.

Bri waved the towel harder and harder. It snapped against the smoke detector, and the plastic cover fell to the floor with a clatter. The smoke detector still didn't cut off.

Beep-beep-beep.

Piper started to shriek, her shrill voice almost as loud as the alarm. Bri waved the towel even harder and started to lose her balance. She teetered on the edge of the chair, arms pinwheeling.

And that's when David came home.

"What's going on?" he yelled over the alarm.

Bri tumbled to the floor but managed to land on her feet. "It's nothing," she told him. Turning to Piper, she said, "It's okay, sweetie."

"She started a fire," Elijah yelled to his brother.

"Not a fire. Just a little smoke." She opened the oven so David could see the smoking wings, shut it again, and went back to waving the dishtowel at the alarm—without climbing back on the chair. David grabbed another towel and helped her. Finally, the blaring stopped.

David swung Piper up in his arms and gave her a twirl. Immediately, she stopped crying and started giggling.

"I made five-spice wings. I used the recipe from a boy who won *MasterChef Junior*," she said to David.

"I want peanut butter," Elijah said.

"I'm on it, dude," David said. Holding Piper under one arm, he grabbed peanut butter, jelly, and bread and quickly made a sandwich. He cut off the crusts, cut the sandwich into four squares, stuck them on a plate and handed it to Elijah. "What about you, Pipes? PB and B?" he asked, grabbing a banana.

Piper nodded, and David set her down.

"Don't you want to try the chicken we made together, Piper?" Bri asked. "You could have some too, David." Wings could have a smoky flavor. They'd still taste good. She hoped.

Piper shook her head. She wrapped herself around one of David's legs as he made her sandwich. It was like she'd forgotten Bri had been giving her piggyback rides about ten minutes before.

David let Piper hang on to him as he made her a peanut butter and banana sandwich.

You're here. He's here. It's all good, Bri told herself. She snatched the can of whipped cream off the counter. Her dad had said if you put cream in a nitrous oxide foamer, the cream would come out like it did from a spray can, so Bri figured whipped cream would work for the part of the recipe that said to put cream in the foamer thing.

She squirted some of the whipped cream into a bowl. It seemed wrong to dip wings in whipped cream and chili, but that's what the recipe said. And the recipe came from the kid who actually won the contest. That kid would know what he was doing. Bri added a dollop of salsa on top of the whipped cream.

"David, do you want to try the wings? You can dip them in this." She held out the bowl. He stared at it, stared at her, and then stared at the bowl again.

"Uh, no thanks," he finally said.

"How about some rice?" She whipped the lid off the pan.

"It's black," David said.

"Yeah." Bri could tell he thought it looked gross. "It, um, has a mild, nutty flavor."

"I'm not that hungry," he told her. "I'm here to stay, so you can go now."

"I'll tell my mom to come get me," Bri said, her shoulders slumping.

"You're in my math class, right?" David asked when she finished texting her mom.

"And social studies," Bri said.

"Sorry, what's your name again?"

He. Didn't. Even. Know. Her. Name. Bri felt as if she'd just swallowed that whole pan of disgusting rice goop. "Bri. Brianna Wei."

"Oh, right. Bri," David said. "I'm new this year. Still getting everyone's names down."

She didn't think he'd forgotten her name. She was sure he'd never known it at all. He was just being nice.

She figured he'd remember now.

Great pretty-much-first impression, Bri, she told herself.

Bring a few first-aid supplies with you when you babysit so you don't have to hunt through cabinets and drawers if there's an accident. Kids especially love bandages with cartoon characters on them.

Chapter 6

"It was horrible. Horrible, horrible, horrible," Bri moaned to Lily the next day. She'd gone over to her friend's house right after breakfast the morning after what would be forever known as the Night of Humiliation. They'd both flopped down on Lily's bed, because Bri insisted she needed to lie down before she could tell Lily what happened.

"I can't believe he didn't know your name," Lily said.

"Well, now that he does, I wish he didn't!" Bri pulled a pillow off Lily's bed and pressed it over her face. "Do you think my parents will let me home school?" she asked, her words coming out muffled.

Lily yanked the pillow away. “Don’t be crazy. It’s not as embarrassing as the time you didn’t realize your skirt was tucked into your underpants after you went to the bathroom and everyone saw your Wonder Woman Underoos.”

“That was in the third grade.”

“Well, yeah,” Lily answered. “But it was pretty bad. Almost as bad as last year when I was halfway up to the stage to accept the Citizenship Award before it registered that they’d called Lily Norquist and not me.”

“Are you going to tell me embarrassing things happen to everyone and David’s probably already forgotten about my—” Bri’s cell rang, interrupting her.

"It’s Mrs. Massey,” she squeaked, looking at the screen. “Do you think I’m going to get fired for nearly torching the house? Which I didn’t. But it might have sounded like I did.”

“Take a deep breath, then answer,” Lily advised.

Bri did as Lily suggested. Mrs. Massey didn't sound mad. "I was hoping you could sit for us tomorrow night," she said.

"Of course!" Bri exclaimed, relief whooshing through her. "Just tell me what time, and I'll be there!"

She grinned at Lily after she finished the conversation and hung up. "This is so perfect. I'm sitting for the Massey's again tomorrow! I'll find a way to make such a good impression it will knock the memory of the Night of Humiliation right out of David's head."

Bri clicked open her calendar and groaned. "Except I already told Mrs. Rankin I'd sit for her."

"Oh, no!" Lily exclaimed. "Well, at least you'll be over at the Massey's again on Wednesday. That's not very far off."

"But it gives the memory days to burn itself into David's brain," Bri answered. "I need to make a new impression fast!" She sat up and brushed her dark hair away from her face. "I'm just going to have to tell Mrs. Rankin I'm sick," she said firmly.

She got ready to hit the Rankin's speed dial number, but her finger wouldn't move. Just thinking about lying to Mrs. Rankin made her feel like she actually was sick, her stomach all queasy. "I can't do it. I've been babysitting for Mrs. Rankin almost since McCoy was born. And it was so great of her to give my info to Mrs. Massey."

Bri was afraid she wouldn't be able to force the words *I can't come on Sunday* out of her mouth, so she wrote a quick apology text to Mrs. Massey instead of calling her back.

Lily studied Bri for a moment then said, "So, what's the next thing on the list we're going to try?"

Hearing Lily say the word *we* made Bri feel better. She gave her friend a fast hug. "I know it's a lot of trouble, and I know you think my whole plan is dumb, but David is so worth it." She rushed on, her words smashing into each other because she was talking so fast. "I told you how cool he was about everything. He didn't say the food looked gross. He just said he wasn't hungry."

"Points for politeness," Lily said.

"And he got the kids ready for bed while I cleaned up the kitchen." Bri didn't mention that there was a possibility that David had made himself busy with the kids so he wouldn't have to stay in the same room with her.

"Points for that too," Lily said.

"So you're admitting that he's someone worth having a crush on," Bri said.

"I never said he wasn't," Lily told her "All I ever said was that you haven't even given him the chance to like the actual you. Maybe he would."

"But you're still going to help me with the list. You just said so," Bri reminded her.

"Yes, I'm still going to help, which makes me as nutso as you are," Lily answered. "I guess that's why we're friends."

Bri pulled up the list on her phone, even though she knew it by heart.

MasterChef Junior, anime, Just Us Folks, marathons.

Marathons. That sounded simple. It was just running, and she knew how to run. There were no ingredients to buy. Nothing to burn. Bri started to feel a little better. She stood up. "My presence is requested for errands right now, but how would you feel about going running with me tomorrow?"

"We should do some stretching first," Lily said when she and Bri reached the track Sunday afternoon. Bri had wanted to run on the school track instead of around the neighborhood just in case David used the track for his runs. How great would it be to see him there? It would be so easy to start up a conversation. The Night Of Humiliation wouldn't even come up, because they'd be so busy talking about how they both loved running.

But the only people on the track were two ladies in matching pink visors doing some slow jogging. That didn't mean David wouldn't show up before Bri and Lily were done, though. Bri was planning to get in nine miles. She'd found a marathon training plan online, and it said to run nine miles on Sunday. She'd chosen the plan for intermediate runners because she wanted to get to David's level fast. If marathons were one of his favorite things, he had to be at least at the intermediate level.

She put one foot on the second row of bleachers and leaned over her leg, joining Lily in her stretching. Lily ran laps with her field hockey team every day before practice. But Bri couldn't remember the last time she'd done any running. It was probably the beginning of last year when Ms. Hahn made the P.E. class run a few laps because they hadn't been paying attention.

But it didn't matter that it had been a while for Bri. Running was running. It's not like you needed lessons on how to do it. Bri stretched out the other leg and looked over at Lily. "Ready?"

"Ready," Lily answered. They walked out to the track and started jogging. Bri's gym shoes were in her gym locker, so she was wearing her Vans. They were flat and had rubber soles—and they were cute, which was critical in case of a David sighting—so she figured they'd be fine. But by the start of the second lap, she felt a blister coming up on the top of the big toe of her left foot.

Who cared? A blister was no big thing. Not if it led to having a great conversation with David.

Two blisters is no big thing either, she decided as she felt a second blister forming on the bottom of the pinky toe on the same foot about halfway into the third lap.

"Are you okay?" Lily asked when they passed the bleachers for the third time.

"Yeah. Fine," Bri answered breathlessly. "Why?"

"You're running kind of . . . off-balance."

Bri focused on her gait and realized Lily was right. She was favoring her right foot because of the blisters on her left. And now a blister was starting on the big toe of her *right* foot.

Blisters smisters, she told herself. *David's worth it.*

"I'm fine," she told Lily again. "Fine," she said one more time, as if that would make her feet feel better.

Fine, fine, fine, she chanted to herself all the way around the fourth lap. "One mile down!" she called out as she and Lily passed the bleachers again. *Eight more to go,* she thought. She couldn't stop herself from groaning.

But she should be getting a runner's high really soon. An article said when your body reached a certain level of discomfort while running, your brain produced a blast of feel-good chemicals that were like natural pain-killers. As soon as it kicked in, she'd be able to run forever. She'd forget all about those blisters. All four of them. Another one had formed on the little pinky on her right foot.

Now that I have two blisters on each foot, it will be easier to run with my weight balanced, Bri told herself. It's all good. *Good, good, good,* she silently chanted as she ran.

After the fifth lap, she changed the chant to *Da-vid, Da-vid, Da-vid.* That kept her going. That was all the motivation she needed. She didn't need a runner's high. She had a David high! *Da-vid, Da-vid, Da-vid!*

"Woo! Two miles!" Lily puffed as they finished the eighth lap. She veered toward the bleachers.

"Where are you going?" Bri called. "We're not even halfway done."

Lily veered back over to Bri. "Exactly how many miles are you planning to do today?"

"David's into . . . marathons. My marathon-training plan says I should do nine miles today," Bri answered, gasping for breath every few words.

"But you've got to build up to it," Lily protested. "You've done enough. At least I've been running a few miles every field hockey practice. You never run."

"In Mrs. Hahn's . . . class," Bri protested.

"One time!" Lily answered. She'd been in the class too.

"I'm doing . . . nine," Bri said. "You . . . do . . . what . . . you . . . want."

After running two more laps with Bri, Lily slowed to a walk. "I'm walking one more lap. Then I'm out. You should stop too."

Bri shook her head, not wanting to waste breath on words. *Da-vid, Da-vid, Da-vid.* On her tenth lap, she had to shift her weight to her heels to take the pressure off her blisters—all seven of them. And now a new blister seemed to be forming right on top of the first one on her right big toe. Was that even possible?

She pushed the blisters out of her head. *Da-vid, Da-vid, Da-vid.*

When Bri passed the bleachers again, Lily was waiting with a bottle of water. "Take some," she urged. Bri shook her head. She was afraid if she slowed down, she'd end up stopping completely. And if she stopped, she didn't think she'd be able to get herself going again.

You'll be able to have a great conversation with David about pushing through the pain to get the miles in, she told herself. *Da-vid, Da-vid, Da—*

A bolt of agony exploded in her left heel, shooting up the back of her leg all the way to her thigh.

She went down. Hard.

"Da-vid Mas-sey," she whispered. But even that wasn't enough to get her back on her feet.

Babysitting jobs won't always go as planned. One of the most important things you can do is keep your sense of humor!

Chapter 7

A knock came on Bri's bedroom door on Monday morning. "You're going to be late for school," her mom said as she opened the door.

"I can't go," Bri answered from where she sat on the floor. She gestured to the huge pile of shoes next to her, every single pair from her closet. "I tried on all of them, and they all murder my feet."

Her mother looked back and forth from the shoe pile to Bri. "I have an idea. Be right back."

"Unless your idea is a double foot amputation, it's not going to work," Bri muttered after her mom left the room. Her mother should know that nothing would work. Lily had been forced to call her to drive them home from the track the day before. Her mother had seen how much pain Bri was in.

"Here!" her mother called triumphantly as she came back into Bri's room, holding a pair of truly horrendous black sneakers over her head.

"Those are the ugliest shoes I've ever seen," Bri blurted out.

"They are also the most comfortable," her mother answered. "They have tons of room for your toes. I bet they won't press on your blisters at all."

"Where did you even get them?" Bri would remember if she'd ever seen anything that awful on her mother's feet.

Her mom smiled at her. "They're all I wore the last three months I was pregnant with you," she answered. "My feet were so swollen, but it still felt like I was walking on clouds."

"They're going to be too big. I wear a half a size smaller than you do," Bri reminded her mother. She'd often wished she and her mom wore the same size. Her mom had some gorgeous shoes that Bri would have loved to borrow.

Not these. Bri didn't even think they should be called shoes. They were more like hoof covers for a Clydesdale.

"Already thought of that." Her mother shook two pairs of Bri's dad's tube socks with her other hand.

Bri squeezed her eyes shut so she didn't have to see the footwear freak show. "My leg is still really hurting too," Bri said. "I really think I have to stay home. Lily can get my homework for me."

"I found this in the medicine cabinet." Her mom pulled a tube of liniment out of her pocket. "I'd forgotten we have it. When I sprained my back planting all those daffodils last year, it took all the pain away. It should do the same for your leg." She tossed the tube to Bri.

"Doctor Murphy's Molten Lava." She looked at her mother. "Molten Lava? That sounds like it would make my leg hurt even more."

"It just feels nice and warm," her mother promised. "Now get a move on. I'll drive you and Lily to school."

"Maybe David and I can bond over running injuries. What do you think?" Bri asked Lily after Bri's mom had dropped them off at school.

"That's actually a good idea," Lily answered. "So are you going to say anything about the . . . you know . . . cooking?"

Bri groaned as she limp-walked toward the school's entrance. "I can't decide. Maybe I could make a little joke about it? Something about how the chicken wings were supposed to taste smoky, but not quite that smoky? Or maybe it would be better not to say anything to remind him of what happened."

"A joke could be good. It would show him you have a good sense of humor and that you don't think it was any big thing," Lily said.

"Hey, girlsies." Megan called as she caught up to them. She launched into her usual mass of questions. "How did it go with the recipes, Bri? Did you impress David? Was he even there? Did the kids eat the stuff?" She crinkled her nose. "What's that smell? Does it smell like a stable to you?"

"You can smell it?" Bri asked. "Even through my jeans? It's this liniment my mom had me put on my leg. I thought I was still smelling it, because a little was left on my fingers."

"What did you do to your leg? Does that stuff help? What's in it, anyway?" Megan asked. "Seriously, the smell makes me think I'm about to go to my riding lesson. Kind of like a sweaty horse."

"But with menthol mixed in," Lily added, giving Bri an apologetic smile. "But it's not that bad. You can only smell it a little," she added quickly.

More than a little, otherwise Megan wouldn't have said anything, Bri thought. This was bad.

This was epically bad. Not only did her feet look like Clydesdale hooves stuffed into sneakers, but she smelled like a horse that had been rubbed down with menthol. And math class—with David—was first period.

The first bell rang as they walked inside. "I'm going to go wash it off really fast," Bri told her friends.

Maybe today wasn't the day to talk to David. But didn't she at least have to say hi? Wouldn't it be weird not to, after he dealt with her cooking catastrophe on Friday? Maybe she should just say hi and thanks again. She could try to start up a conversation about running in a few days when she was wearing her own super-cute shoes. Or maybe today she could just get away with not actually speaking to him at all. She could just give him a really friendly smile.

Bri was so caught up in strategizing that she walked—well, limped—right past the bathroom. She was almost to the door of her math class before she realized her mistake. She checked the clock over the bulletin board. Three minutes to the second bell. She should be able to make it. She spun around—and almost slammed into David.

"You!" she exclaimed, before she could stop herself. "Hi there, you!" she said, trying to make the "you!" sound like it had been intentional. And normal. "Those smoky wings were pretty smoky, huh?"

He didn't answer, and Bri realized he was staring at the ground. No, not the ground! Her shoes! Her massive, ugly shoes. "I know my shoes are really repellent, but I kind of messed up my feet. Running."

She took her math book and binder out of her backpack just so she'd have something to do with her hands. They felt weird just hanging there at her sides. "I left my running shoes in my locker, and ran in my Vans. Rookie mistake. I should know better. But I wanted to stick to my schedule. Prepping for a marathon," she added. She'd been talking about her schedule for converting herself into David's perfect girl, but she wasn't telling him that!

She started to switch her binder from one hand to the other, but her palms were sweaty, and it slipped out of her hands.

"Got it," David said. He bent down. The position put his nose right at liniment level. He was going to get a huge whiff.

Bri jerked back—and managed to whack David in the nose with her knee. "Sorry! I'm so sorry!" she exclaimed. "I didn't want you to—"

There was no way to finish that thought. She couldn't say she didn't want him to think she smelled disgusting.

David straightened up, rubbing his nose. He handed Bri her binder. "No prob. Class is about to start. We should get in there, Bri."

Well, he remembered she was in his math class. And he'd remembered her name. And he'd been nice to her even after she'd kneed him in the nose. It was an above-and-beyond kind of niceness. *I'm making . . . progress,* Bri told herself with a queasy-making mix of shame and elation.

They'd laugh about it all—the Clydesdale hoof covers, the stink, the nose injury, the fire alarm. They'd think the way they got to know each other was the funniest thing ever.

Someday.

The American Red Cross offers a class called Babysitter's Training with Pediatric First Aid/CPR. Taking it prepares you for emergencies and gives parents an extra reason to hire you.

Chapter 8

"Tonight I'm going to rally," Bri told her friends at lunch on Wednesday afternoon. "I even listened to Folks Like Us in my sleep."

"Oh, good idea," Sophie said, opening her cranberry juice.

"When we quizzed you on the lyrics yesterday, you got almost ninety percent right," Abby added.

"Okay, I've been trying not to say this for days. I want to be supportive. Really. But how can you still be going through with this plan to turn yourself into what's basically the anti-Bri? Your mom and I had to practically carry you off the track on Sunday. You could have ended up on crutches for months. You could have ended up wearing those massive boots with all those thick Velcro straps, which are a million times uglier than your mom's pregnancy shoes!"

"I'm not going to injure myself by playing some music and talking to David about it," Bri protested. How could Lily be trying to make Bri quit Project David? She knew how important it was to Bri, and Lily was supposed to be her best friend.

"If I had a list of stuff Christopher Lakshmin liked, I'd be doing the same thing," Abby said.

Bri looked at Lily. "See?"

"What you have planned for tonight really doesn't sound dangerous. Just some music and possible conversation," Sophia said. She looked over at Lily, who gave a tiny shrug.

"Did you talk to him in math today?" Megan asked. "Are you going to talk to him in social studies? Or will tonight be the first time you're going to talk to him since you almost broke his nose?" She tapped her nose with one of her French fries.

"I didn't almost break his nose!" Bri cried. "There might have been one drop of blood. That's all. And he said it was no prob." She sucked in a deep breath and answered Megan's questions. "I haven't actually talked to him since. I've smiled at him a few times. And he smiled back. I'm sure tonight when he hears me playing Folks Like Us, he'll say something about how they're one of his faves, and we'll have a nice, normal conversation. Even if we talk for just thirty seconds, it's all good. Thirty normal seconds talking about something we both like will be definite progress."

"You mean something he likes a lot and you don't like at all," Lily mumbled.

"I don't *not* like them," Bri protested.

"That's what you should say tonight. 'David, I don't not like that group you love,'" Lily said. Bri thought Lily meant it to be a joke, but it hadn't come out sounding jokey.

Sophia reached into her bag and pulled out a little bottle of perfume. "I thought you might want to borrow this for tonight. It's called Deliciously Kissable Love Potion. It smells kind of like caramel and berries and chocolate. So you won't smell anything like liniment. And you'll make David think of really yummy food, not . . . other food. I sprayed some on my note to Jacob Latimer," she confessed

"Soph! Thank you!" Bri exclaimed, reaching over to give her friend a half hug. She couldn't help but think Sophia was acting more like a best friend than Lily was.

Bri checked the clock. 8:45. David should be home pretty much any minute. She figured practice ended about seven or seven-thirty. He was probably hanging with other guys on the team, but it was a school night, and they'd all have to be getting home soon.

She adjusted the volume on the speakers. The music couldn't be too loud with the kids in bed.

But it needed to be loud enough for David to register she was listening to Folks Like Us.

She reached for her phone to text Lily but put it right back in her pocket. It was automatic for her to text Lily about everything, but she didn't want another lecture on how Project David was a bad idea.

Maybe she should text Sophie. She'd been so supportive, loaning Bri that perfume. Lily just didn't understand because she'd never liked someone—not the way Bri liked David. Even though the guy Sophie liked was an actor she'd probably never meet, she got it.

Bri got her phone out again. She'd just pulled up the contacts when she heard a key turning in the lock.

Bri reclined casually on the sofa and then sat up fast. That felt a little too casual. She put her feet on the coffee table and quickly whipped them off again. Way too casual. She crossed her legs and tried to get an I'm-so-into-this-song expression on her face. It was kind of hard. She just wasn't a folk-y girl. And this song, for some reason, had an accordion. An accordion! Did anyone under twenty really listen to accordion music?

She heard footsteps in the entryway. One set of footsteps. It had to be David and not his parents!

David stepped into the living room. "Oh, hi." His eyes darted around the room, not landing on Bri's face. "I'm home, so you can take off."

He hadn't even noticed the music. He definitely hadn't gotten close enough to smell the Deliciously Kissable Love Potion. Bri needed more time.

But what could she do? He'd basically told her to go. She couldn't just keep sitting there like a lump.

At least she'd have a few more minutes before one of her parents could get there to drive her home. Maybe he'd realized his favorite group was playing before they arrived. Maybe he'd even get a whiff of caramel and chocolate. Everybody loved that smell.

"I just have to call for a ride," Bri said. She had her home number on speed dial, but she started punching in the whole thing to give herself some extra seconds.

"Is this Folks Like Us?" David asked just before Bri hit the last number.

She hung up and tried not to break into a ridiculously big grin. "It is. I love them." Even though she didn't love them, she thought David loving them was adorable. All their songs were really romantic, which meant he had to be really romantic too.

"What do you like about them?" David asked, sitting down on the arm of the sofa.

He's within perfume-smelling distance, Bri thought, heart pounding. *Keep calm,* she ordered herself. *You prepped for this.*

"The way their voices fit so perfectly. It's like they're pieces in a puzzle." Abby had helped her come up with that one. Her friends—well, except for Lily—had been great about helping her prep for this moment. They'd spent almost three lunch periods talking about Folks Like Us. Lily hadn't helped at all. She'd just sat there, saying almost nothing. It was like she was on strike against Project David.

David nodded. "Have you ever seen them in concert?"

Bri wanted to say yes, but she thought that she might end up getting caught in a lie. "I wish," she answered. "I heard at their concerts they talk about how they ended up falling in love and getting married."

"Do you watch the vids their fans put up?" His sky-blue eyes gleamed with interest. The band had tweeted, asking their fans to post clips of themselves singing the song "Hearts with Wings" in the most romantic place they knew.

"For sure," Bri answered. "My favorite was that one with the couple in the horse-drawn carriage. The way the horse kept staring at them as they sang? It cracked me up," Bri answered. She actually had liked that one, but she'd gotten really sick of hearing "Hearts with Wings." Even if she'd loved the song, she would probably be sick of it by now, but she didn't even like it that much. David was worth it, though.

David fiddled with the little plastic thing at the end of his shoelace. "So, you check out all the Vine stuff?"

"I'm always looking to see if there's something new," Bri said. Which was totally true—if you only counted the days since she'd abandoned her attempt to become a marathoner.

"They both play so many instruments. I haven't even heard of all of them. Like I read she plays a dulcimer. I'm not even sure what that is," David admitted. "Are you?"

Dulcimer. Dulcimer. It sounded kind of familiar. Sorta kinda familiar. But there was no way she'd be able to tell him what one was.

Sweat popped out on her palms the way it had that day outside math class when she'd dropped her binder and ended up slamming her knee into David's nose. Dulcimer. How could she not know what a dulcimer was? She felt like she might be about to have a heart attack. She'd taken that class on pediatric CPR, but the instructor hadn't explained how to do it on yourself.

She jumped up. "I . . . I need to go check on the kids." She hurried off before he could say anything and ducked into Piper's room. The little girl was sleeping under a mound of stuffed animals. Bri smiled. She was so cute.

She went to pull her phone out of her pocket so she could google "dulcimer." But it wasn't there. She must have left it on the coffee table.

Maybe it wasn't such a big deal that she didn't know what a dulcimer was. Even huge fans of a band didn't know everything about their music. David was a fan and he didn't know what a dulcimer was. If he didn't, it shouldn't be a big thing that she didn't. She smoothed her hair and started for the bedroom door but then hesitated.

What if David asked her other questions?

It wouldn't seem that strange if she didn't know a few things about Folks Like Us. But if he kept asking things she couldn't answer, he'd figure out she was a complete faker.

She sank down on the floor. There was only one thing to do. Hide in here and avoid David.

It was all good, though. She'd had an actual conversation with him. She'd established that they both loved the same group. And nothing horrible had happened!

Tonight definitely counted as a success.

Make sure you know parents' rules about TV. How much TV? Homework done first? Any shows or channels off-limits?

Chapter 9

"Today's assignment is to turn me into a full-on ultimate horror movie fan before Friday," Bri announced Friday at lunch. "I want to know everything I should know. I don't want to have to hide like I did last night." She'd already told her friends about her success in showing David that they both loved Folks Like Us, even though she'd had to bolt when he asked that dulcimer question.

"You should probably specialize in one kind of horror movie," Abby said. "There are way too many to learn about all of them."

"Maybe someone would like to talk about something other than Project David for once," Lily muttered.

What was Lily's problem? She didn't want to help Bri anymore—fine. But the other girls were having fun. They wanted her to be happy, even if Lily didn't.

"I don't mind helping," Sophie said. "Unless—did you have something you wanted to talk about, Lily?"

Lily shrugged. "No. Just thought it was worth checking. Since there are five of us at the table."

"You don't even have something you want to talk about after you made a thing about it?" Bri demanded. "I don't get you. The plan is finally starting to work. Are you jealous or something because your Love Goddess hasn't sent you the perfect guy? Or any guy at all?"

The words had flown out of Bri's mouth before she could stop them. A stunned silence swept over the table. Bri swallowed hard. She'd been too harsh, even though Lily was being so un-bestie. Finally, Bri took a deep breath and spoke, "Lils, I'm sorry. I shouldn't—"

"I have to go to the library," Lily interrupted. She jerked to her feet, swinging her backpack onto one shoulder. "I have an actual project to work on. For school."

The remaining girls looked awkwardly at each other. Megan finally asked, "So what should be your specialty? Classic stuff like Frankenstein? Zombies? Ones with teen characters?"

"I . . . I haven't thought about it," Bri said, struggling to bring her attention back to becoming a horror movie expert. Should she go after Lily?

"I found something on a horror genre wiki page," Abby said, holding up her phone. "You said anime was on the list, right?"

Bri nodded. All her other friends were still willing to help her. If Lily wasn't, that was her problem. Maybe she really was jealous. She was always talking about her Love Goddess. Maybe she couldn't deal with Bri getting a chance at love before she did.

She looked over at Abby and managed to smile. "Yep, anime was on there."

"So you should do Japanese horror," Abby announced. "It's not anime, but it shows you're interested in Japanese culture."

"It's a two-for-one. Great idea," Sophie said. Her eyes flicked to the doors of the cafeteria, like she was waiting for Lily to come back.

Bri wanted to look at the doors too, but she wouldn't let herself. "Perfect idea," Bri said. "Thanks, Abby. I think I should make flashcards. Would you be up for doing directors for me?" Abby nodded. "Sophie, will you do actors?"

"It's dangerous to let Sophie do actors," Abby joked. "She'll end up on a Jacob Latimer page and never leave."

"I won't. I promise." Sophie crossed her heart.

"Megan, can you do the most popular movies?" Bri asked. Megan nodded. "I'll do the history part," Bri said. She cleared her throat. Her voice kept coming out all shaky. "I also want to pick a movie to be watching after the kids go to bed. Something that will show David I'm a fan."

"Are you sure you'll be able to watch one without freaking out? Remember the Lost Dutchman Mine ride," Sophie said.

"That was a long time ago," Bri answered.

"I think it was last summer," Abby said.

"Maybe, but a movie isn't as scary. Nothing pops right out at you, like on the ride," Bri said. Not that she really believed that movies weren't as bad. She wouldn't even stay in the room if a commercial for a horror movie came on.

"I guess you can just grab onto David if you get scared," Sophie added. "That could be fun."

"Really fun." Bri pulled some index cards out of her purse and handed different colors to each of her friends. "I was serious about needing flashcards. I have less than three days to prep."

"Don't worry. We'll make sure you're ready in time," Sophie said.

Bri believed Sophie. So why did she feel like someone had just pulled her chair out from under her?

"Okay, Elijah, bedtime," Bri announced. *Finally!* It felt like it had taken eons for eight-thirty to roll around. She was so excited about the possibility of another bonding session with David. So excited she was almost able to forget that Lily had been avoiding her since Monday. Lily hadn't even been eating at the lunch table with all their friends. Sophie said Lily told her that she needed to spend time on her homework and was going to eat in the library for a while.

This was not the time to be thinking about Lily. Wednesday night had been so great (except for the dulcimer and the hiding).

Tonight would be even better.

She'd gone over the flash cards dozens of times. She was fully prepped. She'd be able to answer anything David asked about Japanese horror. Even if Japanese horror turned out not to be one of his faves, she'd still get points for being a horror fan.

"I'm not tired," Elijah said. It sounded like a declaration of war.

"You don't have to go to sleep," Bri told him. "But you do need to get in bed. You can read or listen to music or—"

"That's boring," Elijah interrupted.

"You didn't let me finish." It was a struggle for Bri to keep the impatience out of her voice. David could be home any second. "How about doing some drawing? I have some great glitter pens and some big sheets of paper." She reached for her Poppins bag. "You know what can be fun? Drawing some pictures of things you've done during the day." That was a baby-sitting tip she'd read online, and it had worked great with other kids Elijah's age.

"That's boring too," Elijah told her.

She recognized his tone. He wasn't going to like any idea she came up with. At least not right now.

"Okay, I understand you don't want to be in bed when you're not tired, but your parents told me your bedtime is eight-thirty. How about, as a special treat, you stay up an extra fifteen minutes?" Bri offered. Sometimes it helped to bend the rules just a little. "How about we have a little snack? I like a bowl of Cheerios before bed some nights." She'd found having something light to eat helped some kids get ready to fall asleep.

"I want cookies," Elijah answered.

Sugar was not going to help the situation. "We could mix together some Cheerios and nuts and a few raisins," she suggested. "It's like homemade trail mix and the raisins make it sweet."

"You said I could have a snack. I want cookies," Elijah insisted.

"One cookie and a glass of milk. Then you are off to bed," Bri said firmly, although she knew she should say no to any cookies at all.

To her relief, Elijah followed her to the kitchen. After his snack, he brushed his teeth again and got into bed. *Super Babysitter does it again!* Bri thought. It was only 8:45. David wasn't home yet. Her plan for the night could still go perfectly.

She turned off Elijah's light, made sure the nightlight was on, told him good-night, and left the room, closing the door quietly behind her. After rushing back to the living room, she turned on the TV. The Masseys had a Roku and had told her she could use their Netflix account. She found *Pulse* and started it up. She wanted to be at least a little way in before David came home.

She'd only watched a few minutes when Elijah loudly called, "Still. Not. Sleepy." Bri jumped up and rushed down to his bedroom.

"You're going to wake up your sister," Bri told him. And if that happened, she'd probably still be trying to get both kids back into bed by the time Mr. and Mrs. Massey came home. Disaster.

"I can't sleep," Elijah announced, sitting up and turning on the lamp beside his bedside table.

"You've only been in bed for about three minutes," Bri told him. "No one falls asleep that fast." She mentally reviewed the contents of her Poppins bag. There had to be something.

Got it. "Have you ever heard of Geronimo Stilton?" she asked. Elijah was seven—about the perfect age for stories of the mouse reporter.

"No." Elijah didn't sound interested.

Bri didn't care. "Hang on. I'll be right back." She rushed out to the living room and grabbed her old iPod from the Poppins bag. She had a few kids' books downloaded, including a Geronimo Stilton. She rushed back to Elijah's room. "This has the coolest story on it." She handed the iPod to Elijah. "It's called *The Lost Treasure of the Emerald Eye*. It's about a mouse who finds a treasure map and goes looking for the treasure. It's the favorite book of another boy I babysit."

She hesitated, pretending to think. "But he's nine, so you probably wouldn't like it. In a couple of years, maybe." She reached for the iPod.

Elijah pulled it out of her reach. "I might like it."

"Well, you can try it. If you want," Bri said. "But it might be a little too old for you."

"I want to listen to it," Elijah insisted.

Bri didn't allow herself to smile. She just cued up the book. When Elijah put the ear buds in and laid back down, she shut off the light and returned to the living room. She'd brought a couple of bags of microwave popcorn. She wondered if she should nuke one. Who could resist the smell of freshly-popped popcorn?

But she heard someone coming in before she could start for the kitchen. She dropped down on the couch a few seconds before David walked into the room. Bri hit pause. "Hi. I was just starting to watch *Pulse*. Rewatch it, actually. I'm addicted to J-Horror." She'd learned that's what fans called Japanese horror. "I can finish it up at home, since you're back." She stood up.

"You're watching a horror movie?" David sounded surprised—surprised and interested. "I wouldn't mind watching. You want to stay and watch it with me?"

"Sure," Bri said, glad that she'd managed to keep her voice sounding calm when she was jumping up and down and shrieking with joy on the inside. "Want me to start it over? It's just been on a few minutes."

"That's okay." David dropped down on the couch. Bri sat next to him—definitely close enough for him to smell the Love Potion perfume that Sophie had let her keep. She unpaused the movie.

"People aren't supposed to go through the doors with red tape on them," she explained. "There are supposedly ghosts in those rooms."

David crossed his arms over his stomach and leaned forward, staring at the screen like he was trying to memorize everything he was seeing. He gave a low groan. "So why is he taking off the tape? Why is he going in there?"

Bri swallowed hard. "'Cause he's stupid?" she muttered. She wanted to stop the movie right there. She didn't want to see what was behind the door. Her heart was already beating so hard it felt like it was going to break her ribs, and her stomach was twisting.

She willed herself not to squeeze her eyes shut. David liked horror. She could learn to like it too. There had to be something awesome about it if David liked it.

The guy on the screen walked down a dimly lit hall. There was something written on the wall in red. In blood? Her heart beat even harder. Her stomach kept twisting. There was something down there in the shadows. A woman. She was walking toward the guy. Slowly. Then . . . then it was like she was a puppet and some of her strings had gotten cut. Half her body slumped, but she continued toward him. Lurching toward him. What was she going to do? Bri dug her nails into her jeans.

The guy scrambled back, terrified. The woman kept coming, the way she moved, completely unnatural and so creepy. She reached for him.

"I have to—" David didn't finish the sentence. He jumped up from the sofa and ran for the back hall.

Should she go after him? Bri wondered. His face had looked really pale. She stood up and followed him. When she got partway down the hall, she heard the sound of puking from the bathroom.

She hesitated. Should she go back in the living room? Or should she ask if he was okay?

Her babysitter instincts kicked in. She walked over to the bathroom door and tapped on it. "David? Are you okay?"

He didn't answer right away. Bri thought about knocking again, but before she could, he called, "Yeah. Fine. I . . . must have eaten something bad. I just need a min—"

A scream came from the living room. It was way too loud to be from the TV.

"Elijah!" Bri cried. She raced toward the sound of the horrified screaming. When she reached the living room, she found Elijah staring at a ghost on the TV screen, eyes wide.

Bri hurried over to him, using her body to block the horrifying scene from his sight. "It's okay. It's okay. It's just a movie."

"What's going on?" Bri jerked her head toward the new voice. Mr. Massey. With Mrs. Massey right behind him.

"He just got scared by something on the TV," Bri explained.

Mrs. Massey rushed over and pulled Elijah into her arms. Mr. Massey got a look at the TV screen, and his mouth tightened. In two long strides, he reached the coffee table. He grabbed the remote and turned the TV off.

"What were you letting him watch?" Mr. Massey demanded as Mrs. Massey hustled Elijah out of the room.

"He wasn't watching it. I mean, I certainly wasn't letting him watch it," Bri began to explain. "I was watching it, and he got up and saw it. I'm so sorry."

"You scared the life out of him. I bet he's not going to want to go to bed for weeks," Mr. Massey told her. "I can't believe you had that on when you knew the kids were just down the hall."

"I was watching it too, Dad," David said as he came back into the room, his face still pale. "We both thought the kids were asleep."

"Why didn't you turn it off the second Elijah came in?" Mr. Massey asked, sounding a little calmer.

"I was in the bathroom," David said. "I got sick to my stomach. I ate a bad hot dog or something, and Bri was checking on me. I guess Elijah got down the hall without her seeing him."

Bri nodded. "I didn't see him go by. I'm so, so sorry," she said again.

Mr. Massey ran his hand through his hair. "The same thing could have happened to me. It's not like I never watch things the kids shouldn't see after they're in bed. I shouldn't have yelled at you." He looked over at David and started to laugh.

Bri stared at him. What was there to laugh about? She was glad he wasn't mad any more, but it's not like anything about the situation was funny. Elijah had been thoroughly freaked.

"Bad hot dog?" Mr. Massey said. "I guess you don't want Bri to know the truth." David's face turned red.

"The truth? The truth about what?" Bri asked. What was he talking about?

"Scary movies make him sick. Always have," Mr. Massey explained. "When he was a little kid, we had to take him out of the room during the flying monkeys part of the *Wizard of Oz*. Just telling him to close his eyes wasn't enough."

Bri looked from David to Mr. Massey. She was so confused. David loved horror. It was on his list of favorite stuff. His dad made it sound like he couldn't stand it.

The scene they'd been watching had made Bri's stomach feel like it was trying to crawl out of her mouth too. That's why she always avoided scary things. So why did David like them so much?

A good babysitter models good behavior.

Chapter 10

Bri spotted David standing outside math class on Monday morning. Just standing there by himself, like he was waiting for someone. As she walked down the hall, he looked up, looked right at her, and smiled.

Was he . . . was he waiting for her?

Her heart began to pound almost as hard as it had during that lurching woman-ghost scene in *Pulse*.

"Hey," David said when she'd almost reached him.

"Hi," Bri said, stopping in front of him.

"Hey," he said again, his face starting to turn red. "I just wanted to say that I really did eat something bad on Friday night. I blame the hot dog I got at Curly's. They always leave them rolling around on that grill for hours."

"Yeah, they do. I think one of my friends got sick from one of those hot dogs once," Bri answered.

It was a lie, but it could have happened. "I almost puked myself, and I hadn't even had a hot dog. The only reason I didn't was because I was too busy biting my tongue. I didn't want to scream and wake up the kids."

David laughed. "Why were you even watching it?"

You've got this, Bri told herself. This time, she wouldn't need to run and hide because she couldn't answer his questions. "*Pulse* comes up on a bunch of lists of the best J-Horror. I think the *New York Times* reviewer nailed it when he wrote that the movie has 'a dreamlike dread of the truly unknown.' And it has a theme that is something we all deal with—the isolation you can feel in an over-populated world. I think it explores—"

Suddenly Bri snapped her jaws shut, her teeth clacking together. What was she doing? She didn't sound anything like herself.

Lily was right. She'd been right all along. Even if Bri conned David into believing she was the perfect girl for him, what was she supposed to do? Watch movies that made her sick and listen to music that bored her? Forget about learning to cook dishes she had no interest in eating—like black rice. Or running more than 26 miles in a day—for fun! Just thinking about it made her leg hurt and her toes tingle where the blisters had been.

Was she really going to try to pretend to be a totally different person until, what, the Senior Prom? That was almost six years away.

"Explores what?" David prompted.

"I don't know," Bri told him. "No, actually, I do know. At least I know what about thirty different reviewers and film scholars think. I've only seen about the first ten minutes, and I hated that!"

David's forehead crinkled in confusion. "What are you talking about?"

She might as well tell him the whole truth. There was no way he was ever going to like her now anyway. "The first night I babysat for Elijah and Piper, we played hide-and-seek. I saw a list of your favorite stuff on your desk." She couldn't bring herself to admit she'd gone into his room just to snoop. "I . . . I decided I would try to like it all too." The last bunch of words had come out way too fast, but at least she'd said them.

David's blue eyes darkened. "What? Why?"

Bri looked around to make sure there was no one who could overhear. "Because I like you," she confessed. "I thought if I showed you we had a bunch of stuff in common—the stuff from that list, like *MasterChef Junior* and marathons and Folks Like Us—that maybe you'd like me too."

David took a step away from her. "So you went through my desk and read something you knew was none of your business. And then you lied to my face every time you saw me." His voice was rough. Bri could tell he was furious.

"I didn't lie, exactly," Bri protested.

"How is acting like you like stuff you hate any different?" he demanded.

And she couldn't answer. Because it really wasn't any different at all.

"That's what I thought," David muttered, walking away.

Bri couldn't wait for lunch. She needed some Lily time. Yeah, Lily hadn't backed Project David the way Bri had thought a BFF should. But it had turned out she was right.

As soon as the bell rang at the end of third period, she rushed to the caf, weaving between the people who were walking way too slowly. She was the first one at the usual table. She pulled out her cell and sent Lily a text.

Lily would know Bri had an emergency situation. Bri hoped Lily wasn't so mad at her that she wouldn't come.

"So? How'd it go Friday night? Have you convinced David you're perfect for him?" Megan asked as she dropped her zebra-print lunch bag on the table and sat down.

"I only want to say what happened once," Bri said. She'd break into a million pieces if she had to do it more than that. "Let's wait for everyone else."

"Okay," Megan said. And that was it. Bri felt grateful that her friend realized she couldn't deal with questions.

Sophia and Abby arrived a few minutes later with trays of food. Bri realized she'd forgotten to buy anything for lunch. It didn't matter. She didn't think she'd be able to eat. Every time she thought about that conversation with David outside of math, her stomach hurt.

"What's wrong?" Sophia asked Bri. Sophia always noticed if someone was upset.

"So much," Bri answered. "I'll tell you everything. I just want to wait for Lily."

Sophia nibbled her bottom lip. "I think Lily's eating in the libr—"

"Here she comes!" Abby cried.

Bri whipped her head toward the entrance. Lily was rushing toward them. "What's wrong?" she exclaimed when she was still a few tables away. "Are you okay?" she asked as she threw herself down into the empty chair next to Bri's.

"You came!" Bri felt like it had been a million years since she'd seen Lily.

"The text said 911," Lily answered, without looking Bri in the eye.

"Okay, here's what happened. David was waiting for me before math, and—" Bri began.

Lily didn't let her finish. "This isn't an emergency situation," she said, her voice cold. "I have to go study." She stood up.

"Lils, stay. You were right. I've been so stupid. This morning David and I were having an actual conversation. He asked me why I watch horror, and I had all these things I could say. Thanks to you." She looked around at Sophia, Abby, and Megan. "But suddenly it's like I was outside my body. And I was watching myself spout all this stuff I'd memorized, and I realized I didn't want to spend all the years until the Senior Prom or whatever being a fake."

She sucked in a huge gulp of air and turned to Lily. "So I told him the truth. The whole truth. About the list. About everything." Bri felt tears sting her eyes and blinked fast to get rid of them. "He was really mad. It was better when he didn't even know my name."

"That's so horrible," Sophia breathed.

"You were right all along, Lily," Bri said. "You can tell me you told me so now."

"I told you so," Lily said, but she didn't sound happy about it. "I'm sorry," she added. She sucked in a deep breath, and looked right at Bri. "And you were right too. I was jealous. I didn't want to be, but I was. I want to like someone as much as you like David."

"You will," Sophia said.

"Even better, someone will like you as much as I like David," Bri told Lily. "And you won't have to pretend to be someone else. Because you're awesome."

"You are too!" Lily exclaimed. "I really meant it when I said David was crazy if he didn't like you just the way you are. That wasn't just me being jealous and trying to make you give up on him."

"Thanks, Lils," Bri told her.

"I think all of you are all kinds of amazing. We'll do a group hug later. Now I need Bri to back up a little," Megan said. "So you weren't planning to tell him? You just blurted it out? You just spewed all over him?"

"Yeah," Bri admitted. "You should have seen his face. He hates me now."

"The Love Goddess hasn't forgotten you," Lily promised. "Someday you'll find yourself and a boy laughing at the same thing, maybe something no one else thinks is funny. Or maybe humming the same song. And you'll just know." She smiled. "See? I still believe—for you and me, for all of us."

"Maybe," Bri said. But she didn't care if it never happened. She was done with love.

Before you take a babysitting job, don't be afraid to ask questions about how you'll get home, how many kids you'll be watching, whether you'll be expected to clean or cook, and how late you'll be asked to stay.

Chapter 11

The next day after school, there was a message on Bri's phone. From David. He must have gotten her number from his mom. Should she even open it? She knew how he felt.

But she knew she deserved to read whatever he'd written. Finger shaking, she clicked open the message.

want to talk to you. meet me in the quad before you leave.

This was even worse. He wanted to tell her how horrible she was in person. Well, she owed him that. She texted Lily to tell her not to wait to walk home and headed to the quad. Even though she walked slowly, it felt like she teleported there. She spotted David sitting on a bench under one of the huge oak trees.

Just let him say everything he has to say, apologize, and then you can leave, Bri told herself. "I got your message," she said to David when she reached him.

He stood up. "Good. Okay. So. Good," he answered.

Bri waited for him to go on. It seemed like he was having trouble coming up with the words he wanted to use. Finally he said, "I'm sorry I got so mad at you the other day."

He was apologizing to *her*? Bri hadn't been expecting that. "You should have been mad. I went through your stuff. And you were right about me lying to you. Even when I did something like cooking those stupid chicken wings, I was lying, because I don't cook. I mean, my specialty is making turkey sandwiches. I have a turkey cookie cutter I use to make them turkey shaped. Kids think it's cool."

As soon as the words were out of her mouth, she realized lying to David wasn't the only bad thing she'd done. She'd taken a babysitting job and halfway ignored the kids she was babysitting! Elijah and Piper should have been her top priority, and she'd spent most of her time thinking about David.

"I didn't pay enough attention to your brother and sister," she confessed. "I know kids. I knew they wouldn't want gourmet food, even if I made it perfectly. I didn't do all my usual fun stuff with them either. I'm usually all about the fun. But I was too focused on impressing you. From now on, Elijah and Piper are getting the full-on Super Babysitter treatment. Games, craft projects, turkey-shaped turkey sandwiches, all of it." She sucked in a deep breath. "Thanks for saying sorry but, really, you didn't have to."

Bri turned to leave, but David caught her lightly by the elbow. "I did have to, because I've been doing pretty much exactly the same thing you have," he said. "Or I would have if I got up the guts."

"I don't know what you're talking about," Bri said, easing her arm away.

"That list of what you thought was my favorite stuff? It's actually Chloe Jensen's favorite stuff," David said. "I kind of . . . I like her. Not that I talk to her or anything. But I know some of her friends, and I've been asking questions about her without being all obvious about it, and—"

Bri laughed.

"That's funny?" David demanded.

"Only because I tried to get info from your brother and sister. Picture me interrogating a four-year-old and a seven-year-old," Bri answered, shaking her head.

Now David laughed too. "Anyway, that's how I made the list: from talking to people who know her. I thought if I liked—or if she thought I liked—the same stuff, she'd like me too. I haven't actually tried it yet, though."

"That's why you were asking me questions about Folks Like Us and attempting to watch

Pulse with me," Bri exclaimed. "I thought it was weird one of your favorite things made you vomit."

"Yeah. I hadn't figured out how I was going to deal with that if I tried to watch horror with Chloe," David admitted.

"I have some flashcards you can have," Bri offered. "They cover everything about Japanese horror. You'll still need to research how to control the nausea, though. I also have some liniment that's good if you try prepping for a marathon." She decided she might as well tell him the whole story. "I was wearing it that day I kneed you in the nose. You bent down to pick up my binder, and I thought you might smell its disgusting smell. I backed up fast and—wham."

David rubbed his nose at the memory. "Do you like any of the stuff on the list?" Bri asked. He shook his head. "Me neither," she continued. "My friend Lily kept telling me it was dumb to pretend I did. And I finally accepted she was right. What if my big plan worked and you started liking me—

I mean, if that list had really been stuff you were into. I'd have to keep doing things I didn't like all the time."

"So what kind of movies do you actually like?" David asked.

Bri felt her body tense. What if she gave the wrong answer? What if she picked something David didn't like at all? What if—

Stop, she ordered herself. *This is what got you in trouble in the first place*. "Comedies," she told him. "The stupider the better."

"Epically stupid," David said.

"Exactly," she answered.

"Me too. I'm going to go see that new Kevin Hart movie with some friends this weekend. It looks like it has the potential to be stupid. You want to come?" David asked. "You could invite some people too."

"Yeah," Bri answered. "That would be fun."

Bri and her friends—she'd invited Abby, Sophia, Megan, and, of course, Lily—plus David and his friends filled up almost one entire row in the movie theater. David had ended up sitting next to Bri. She thought maybe he'd done it on purpose. She was pretty sure she'd noticed him nudging one of his friends so it would work out that he'd be in the seat next to hers. Lily was on her other side.

"Love Goddess at work," Lily whispered in Bri's ear. "Sitting next to David at a movie you both actually want to see."

Maybe, Bri thought. How weird it would be if David ended up liking the real Bri. And if Bri ended up liking the actual David. All she really knew about him so far was that he was nice and he liked stupid movies. But those were both good things.

The theater lights dimmed, and the first trailer started. It was for some big action flick. Chris Pratt was having a fight on top of a huge crane in the middle of what looked like a hurricane. Bri gasped when it looked like he was about to fall. A couple of the guys, including David, applauded.

And Lily laughed. So did the boy sitting next to her. They were the only two people in the theater who did.

Bri remembered something Lily had said a few days before. She leaned close so she could whisper in her best friend's ear. "Someday you might find yourself and a boy laughing at the same thing, maybe something no one else thinks is funny."

Lily smiled. "Told you the L.G. was in the vicinity."

Bri was sure Lily was right when David reached over and took Bri's hand.

About the Author

Melinda Metz is the author of more than sixty books for teens and kids, including the YA series Roswell High (basis of the TV show, *Roswell*). She's currently writing a middle-grade series, S.M.A.R.T.S, about kids in a makerspace club who solve mysteries. Melinda lives in Concord, North Carolina, with her dog, Scully, a pen-eater just like the dog that came before her.

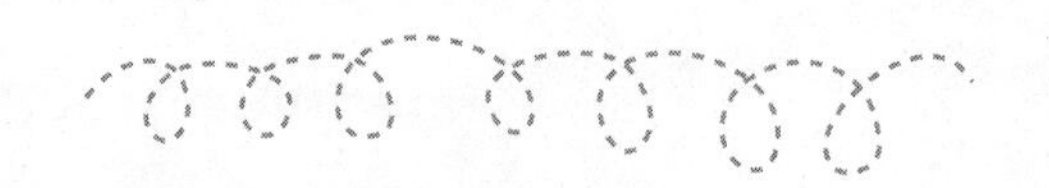

anime (AN-uh-may)—a Japanese style of motion-picture animation that uses highly stylized, colorful art and futuristic settings

catastrophe (kuh-TASS-truh-fee)—a terrible and sudden disaster

declaration (dek-luh-RAY-shuhn)—something that is announced

dulcimer (DUHL-suh-mer)—a modern folk instrument related to the guitar and plucked with the fingers

elation (ih-LAY-shuhn)—a state or feeling of great joy or pride

euphoria (you-FOR-ee-uh)—a strong feeling of happiness

horrendous (hor-REN-duhs)—dreadful and horrible

interrogating (in-TER-uh-gate-ing)—questioning formally and thoroughly

liniment (LIN-uh-mehnt)—a liquid medicine rubbed on the skin especially to relieve pain

repellent (ri-PEL-uhnt)—disgusting

strategize (STRAT-i-jize)—to plan a course of action

substitutions (SUHB-sti-too-shuhns)—things used in place of others

voila (vwah-LAH)—an expression used to show success or satisfaction

Let's Talk!

1. Each chapter in the book begins with a babysitting tip that relates to that chapter. Choose a few of the tips and explain how they relate to what happens in the story.

2. Do you think Bri is a good babysitter? Share examples from the text to support your answer.

3. Bri pretended to be someone she isn't. What kind of problems can that create? Have you ever had a similar experience?

Write About It!

1. Write a character description for the Love Goddess, using both the girls' descriptions in the book as well as your own imagination.

2. Which of the following characters are you most like: Megan, Bri, Lily, Abby, or Sophia? Use specific examples from the text to explain your answer.

3. Write a scene from David's point of view that takes place after Bri tells him the truth about the list. How does he come to realize that he should apologize to Bri?

Routines and Rules

Bri is normally a terrific babysitter. She cares about kids and is responsible and organized. Like Bri, you can create your own index-card system to remember the routines and rules when you babysit. Discuss children's routines and preferences with the parents at the beginning of each job. You should know:

- What meals or snacks should children have? What foods are okay to eat?
- How much TV or electronics time is allowed? At what times?
- What TV shows are children allowed to watch?
- What video games are they allowed to play?
- What other activites are okay?
- When is bedtime? What is the children's bedtime routine?

A parent is likely to write down some of the things you need to know while you're babysitting. It might look something like this.

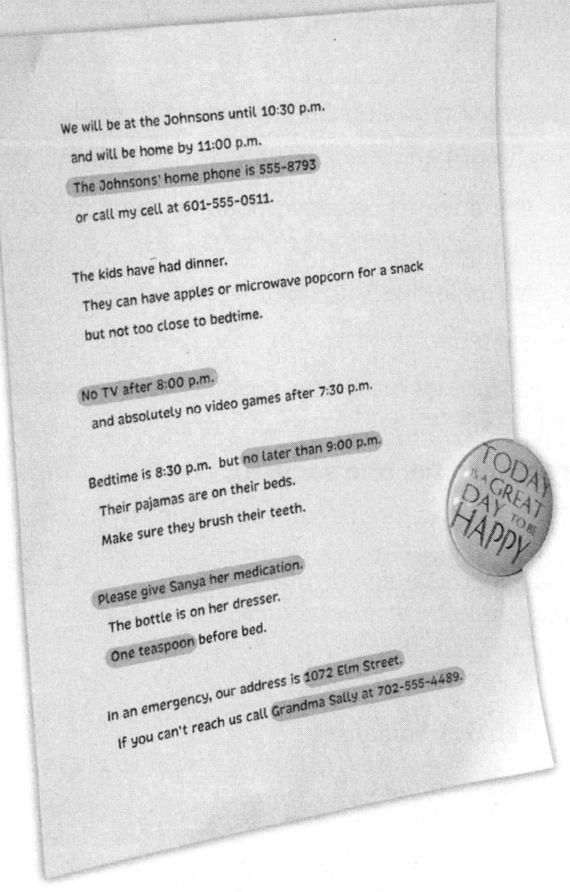

We will be at the Johnsons until 10:30 p.m.
and will be home by 11:00 p.m.
The Johnsons' home phone is 555-8793
or call my cell at 601-555-0511.

The kids have had dinner.
They can have apples or microwave popcorn for a snack
but not too close to bedtime.

No TV after 8:00 p.m.
and absolutely no video games after 7:30 p.m.

Bedtime is 8:30 p.m. but no later than 9:00 p.m.
Their pajamas are on their beds.
Make sure they brush their teeth.

Please give Sanya her medication.
The bottle is on her dresser.
One teaspoon before bed.

In an emergency, our address is 1072 Elm Street.
If you can't reach us call Grandma Sally at 702-555-4489.

Excerpt from *You're in Charge: Basic Rules Every Babysitter Needs to Know* by Melissa Higgins, published by Capstone Press, 2015.

If you have permission from the parents, cooking can be a really fun activity for the kids you babysit. Mini pizzas are sure to be more popular than five-spice chicken wings!

Mini Pizzas

Ingredients for one serving:

- a bagel
- 2 tablespoons pizza or marinara sauce
- 1/4 cup mozzarella cheese
- sliced cherry tomatoes
- sliced black olives

What you do:

1. Split the bagel and toast both halves in a toaster. Place on a baking sheet.
2. Spread a tablespoon of sauce on each half.
3. Add the vegetable toppings.
4. Sprinkle 2 tablespoons of cheese on each half.
5. Broil in oven until the cheese melts. Watch closely to make sure it doesn't burn.

Experiment with different toppings, and if the kids are picky, plain cheese pizzas are sure to please!

Kaitlyn and the Competition

by D. L. Green

Kaitlyn is a top-notch babysitter: she's very organized, disciplined, and efficient. And she needs her regular babysitting gigs to pay for new clothes, bedroom decor, and, of course, her cell phone. So when the Sweet family decides to replace her with a new, fun sitter named Doc, she's determined to beat her new competition . . . if only she could figure out who he is. But will Kaitlyn come to realize that even an experienced sitter like her can learn a thing or two from the new guy on the block?

Elisabeth and the Unwanted Advice

by C. H. Deriso

Elisabeth Caldwell's first babysitting job is coming up none too soon. She needs to earn some cash to buy some new gear for her latest interest, tennis. When her grandma hears that Elisabeth will be babysitting, she offers up a list of advice. Meanwhile, Elisabeth is crushing on a boy, and her best pal has her own list of advice on how to get him. Unfortunately, Elisabeth soon finds out that not all advice is good, embarrassing herself terribly in the process!

Olivia Bitter, Spooked-Out Sitter

by Jessica Gunderson

With the start of seventh grade, Olivia's longtime friend, Beth, has found new interests and new friends. Olivia thinks if she could just afford the type of clothes that Beth now wears, maybe their friendship could be restored. Motivated by a need for cash, Olivia agrees to babysit for a family of four who recently moved to the neighborhood haunted house. Now she's not sure what's scarier: hearing countless creepy sounds or being responsible for four kids!

The fun doesn't stop here!
Discover more at
www.capstonekids.com
• Videos & Contests
• Games & Puzzles
• Friends & Favorites
• Authors & Illustrators
Plus, find cool websites and more books like this one at www.facthound.com.
Just type in the Book ID: 9781496527561
and you're ready to go!